Behind The
MASK

U. E. Wynn

ISBN-13: 978-1-7320325-0-7
ISBN-10: 1732032505

DEDICATION

First and foremost, I would like to thank the creator, The All Eye Knowing, for giving me the knowledge, wisdom, and understanding to prevail through all my atrocities. For allowing me numerous chances to correct the many mistakes throughout this walk called life. For that I am truly humbled and grateful.

As always, both of my mothers, Danette and Toykey for being outstanding and ambitious go-getters. This book has truly been inspired by my little cousin Michael Denzel Wynn, who is more like a little brother and a best friend. Watching him step into fatherhood and doing a fantastic job in pursuing his personal goals, while assisting me in all my endeavors is truly a blessing.

I would also like to thank my little cousin Mari Brooklyn and my twin nieces Adriana and Ayla, who are my pride and joy. To my little sister and business partner Amina, I want to say thank you for the push, motivation and encouragement. This one is also for my sister Jyvonda, my little brother Dante, and my grandmother Iris.

Welcome home to my brother Shane, my true friend Blast and to all my fallen comrades. To my A1 day 1's, and to my team; you know who you are. I love and appreciate each and every one of you. Now let's get to it! To the women that have been sturdy rocks in our friendships, relationships and situationships, I thank you sincerely.

U.E. Wynn
.

ABOUT THE AUTHOR

U.E. Wynn

A self-educated, business savvy, humble entrepreneur was counted out at a young age by his peers, teachers, and family members. After enduring life altering events that would destroy and/or diminish any individual, he chose to overcome and excel. He turned what would be deemed a negative into a positive. He reevaluated himself and reclaimed a positive position within society.

U.E. Wynn is the founder of 501C nonprofit, Save a H.O.M.I.E. Inc. and an active activist within the community. He continues to assist disenfranchised youth, feed and clothe the homeless and bring forth literacy to the illiterate. Wynn also helps in providing a positive, productive and social atmosphere for the youth to unwind and enjoy themselves throughout the Carolinas via events, concerts and parties.

This is Wynn's second novel presenting you with a page turning, nail biting, exotic read.

PROLOGUE

Doug Walsh was talented and comfortably secure financially. Yet, there were missing pieces from his life that he had to fulfill in order to obtain the life that he has always wanted and dreamed of. He was now thirty four years old and experiencing turmoil in each relationship he'd encountered over the years. It was making his life a living hell, even though he had what most people could only dream of.

After finding the woman he thought would become his wife, he later discovered that she was a crack addict who depended on him to support her habit. Wishing he could dismiss her from his life was out of the question and not in the cards, because he soon found out that he was already in too deep. She was pregnant and wreaking havoc amongst various other things he now had to deal with.

As if his life wasn't already complex with all of his new business ventures, it was now in shambles. To make matters worse, he had to cover, shield, and hide his troubles daily from the relationship he had endured in his quest to find true love. He constantly tried finding the real person behind the mask of each and every person he'd met trying to discover who was really sincere.

He devoted his life to detect the truthfulness in others, even though he also wore a mask. He had cards he wasn't showing in hopes to stay one step ahead of everyone else. Never showing his true character, he schemed, connived, and always manipulated others to obtain what he wanted in life. But deep down, he knew it would one day catch up with him. Although he knew he couldn't prevent it from happening, he still made it his business to never reveal who was really behind the mask.

The problem was keeping his friends in the dark from finding out about his secrets. These secrets had destroyed him at an early age and damaged his pride. It had shaped him in ways he didn't understand himself. He didn't want that part of his life reactivated causing him to lose all he had obtained. That's not how he wanted to live his life. But he could never erase how he really felt about his desires or mixed emotions.

He thought back to the day when he was a ten year old kid and what caused him to miss the school bus forcing him to stay home that day.

The phone rang loudly and he yanked it up quickly.

"Hello," he answered.

"Doug, let me speak to your mother. It's your aunt Ruth."

"Oh, hi Auntie. She's not home. She's gone to work," he said.

"I missed her, huh? I really needed to talk to her," she said with a bit of frustration.

"Well, I'll tell her you called when she comes home this evening," Doug responded, trying to rush her off the phone before she realized he shouldn't be home.

"What are you doing home?" she asked concerned.

Damn. "I missed my bus this morning," Doug explained.

"Come over here and stay with me because you don't need to be there in the house alone," she said.

Thinking of eating a good meal and having his auntie as company wasn't such a bad idea, Doug thought.

"Okay, I'll be over in a few minutes," he said.

"Alright. I'll make you some breakfast," she said before hanging up.

Doug cut the TV off and locked the doors before leaving the house to make his way over to his auntie's house. Upon arriving, he thought about what his mother would say at the thought of him missing school. He was somehow hoping that his auntie could ease the tension by talking to his mother in some way or another. As he stepped on the front porch, the door opened and he was greeted by his uncle Sherman who kindly invited him in.

"Hi, Uncle Sherman!" Doug smiled.

"Hey little man. Come on in here. How you doing?" he asked with a wide grin.

"Alright. I missed my school bus this morning," Doug said as a way of explaining why he was there.

"Yeah! Your auntie told me you were on the way over."

Doug heard his auntie call his name. "Doug, come eat this

breakfast," she screamed.

Doug followed his Uncle Sherman into the kitchen where they sat and ate together talking occasionally about whatever came to mind. When the phone rang, his auntie answered it to discover she had to run an errand.

"I've got to go and take some papers to work for them to fill out for me to receive my percentage of the sale," she said.

"Okay, honey," Sherman said and smiled.

"I'll be back in an hour or two, alright Doug? If you need anything, ask your Uncle Sherman and he'll take care of you."

"Thanks Auntie. I'll see you later," Doug said as his auntie strolled out the door to take care of her business. Doug continued eating breakfast with his uncle Sherman, unaware of what was about to take place. It would be something that would disturb and follow him for the rest of his life.

~ ~ ~ ~

After finishing his breakfast, Doug was about to leave the table when his uncle Sherman stopped him. "Doug you want more orange juice?"

"Yes!" Doug, replied. He loved orange juice and usually was only allowed one small glass. Little did he know that this would be the last glass of orange juice he would ever drink following the incident.

His uncle proceeded to pour him some orange juice and secretly slipped a sedative in the glass before he gave it to him. Doug drank the juice none the wiser, as if he was dying of thirst. He never noticed the peculiar taste as it went down. Right afterwards he went into the living room to watch television. A few minutes later he was joined by his uncle Sherman, who sat down beside him on the sofa.

Within seconds he started feeling faint as he sensed a feeling of sleepiness coming on and began to doze off. Suddenly, he felt his clothes being removed and hands in places that didn't feel normal. Yet he couldn't resist because he couldn't move any part of his body to stop what was happening to him. But he knew something wasn't right. Desperately trying to wake from his state of sleepiness, he struggled to move. He now felt pain where he never felt it before. Moaning and hollering was to no avail because all he could manage was a dry muffle. He couldn't scream out for help nor could he stop what was taking place. He was all alone with no one to help him.

~ ~ ~ ~

At the gas station his auntie Ruth noticed she left an important document and had to return home to retrieve it. After filling the tank in her car, she doubled back home and went into the house only to be shocked at the sight of her husband violently penetrating her nephew.

"What the hell are you doing?" she screamed at him.

Shocked by the sound of her voice, he jumped up naked and ran out of the living room.

Ruth hurried over to Doug and turned him over. She noticed that he was incapacitated, unable to move or comprehend what she was saying to him. In a rage, she stormed into the bedroom where her husband was quickly yanking up a pair of jeans. She needed to find out why and what caused him to violate her nephew in that manner.

"Sherman! Why did you do that to him? Are you gay?"

"Shut the hell up! You don't know what you're talking about bitch," he yelled at her with violence in his eyes.

"What am I going to tell my sister?" she screamed angrily.

"You're not going to say anything or I'll kill your ass," he said with a sneer.

Knowing she couldn't let the incident go, she thought furiously about what she should do as her nephew laid there bleeding from his anal in her living room. She had to take action or she could never live it down. Not to mention looking Doug in the eyes ever again.

She told her husband to clean him up while she went to work as planned. He agreed as she proceeded out the door and got into the car. Her mind raced at the shock of seeing a side of Sherman she'd never seen before.

Once she turned the corner, she pulled over and retrieved her cell phone and dialed 911 to report the incident. She then called her sister at work and explained what had taken place. She told her to leave work and meet her at the house because the police were on their way there at that moment.

Ruth then returned home and waited for their arrival. When the police arrived, she explained the incident that had taken place with her husband and nephew. She noticed her sister pulling up minutes later running from the car frantic and furious.

"Where's my son?" she hollered.

"He's in the house with Sherman. The police just got here," Ruth said shakily.

"What the hell is he still in there with that pervert for? Arrest him!"

As the officers surrounded the house both women waited and watched as the officers went to the door. Upon knocking Sherman opened the door shocked to see the police and his wife and sister-in-law standing behind them.

"What's the problem officer?" Sherman asked innocently.

"Sir, you are under arrest for child molestation. You have the right to remain silent. Anything you say can and will be used against you in a court of law. You have the right to an attorney, if you can't afford one, one will be provided for you. Do you understand these rights?"

"Yeah…I understand this is bullshit," he screamed out loud.

"Sherman how could you do this to Doug?" Ruth murmured heatedly.

"You sorry perverted bastard. Why did you molest my son?" Doug's mother screamed angrily as she ran past him making her way to Doug who was still lying on the sofa heavily sedated and virtually unaware of what had taken place.

Noticing the condition of her son and the thought of what happened only made her livid. Anger set in and took control as she looked into the man's eyes while he was being handcuffed. Without warning, she reached into her purse and pulled out a .38 caliber snub nose and pulled the trigger. The bullet hit Sherman directly in the head as blood splattered everywhere.

Out of instinct, the officers all pulled their weapons and ordered her to drop hers. Not caring, she fired two more rounds into his lifeless body before the police fired and killed her on the spot. The incident that was disgraceful now had turned out to be even more tragic in the end.

As paramedics entered to try and revive the bodies they declared both were in fact dead. Doug was taken to Duke Medical Center and treated before being released into his Aunt Ruth's custody. She went on to raise him as her very own after the devastation of losing his mother violently. He never understood what happened that night, but still became scared by it when he was told. He blamed himself and felt he was the cause of his mother losing her life.

Ruth didn't know her sister had set up a college fund for Doug so he could attend college, along with a trust fund that he would acquire at the age of eighteen. The money came from the insurance policy of her late husband who died tragically in the Vietnam War. The large amount he was granted from the policy allows him to live comfortably through life.

Doug, although hampered by the tragic thoughts of what took place in his life, found his way with his Auntie Ruth inspiring and motivating him to achieve higher goals. He's very intelligent with an enormous outlook on what he wanted to obtain even though he knew he couldn't replace what he had lost... his mother's love. But there wasn't a doubt in his mind that he couldn't find what he needed, because he was devoted to filling this void.

Although his Auntie shared every inch of herself it never came close to what was taken away from him. A part of him was gone and left him searching to find it in others that he encountered. This was one fear that he was destined to accomplish as he strived to find truth and sincerity to suffice his fears.

Upon finishing high school and completing college, he moved on with a degree in Business Administration. His first investment was in a night club that he named *Club Palace* which prospered elegantly in its first year. The club brings in an enormous profit and sky rocketed his popularity all over the city. Everyone wanted to go see what was so sensational about *Club Palace* and the man that ran it. He had quickly become a local celebrity that was low-key and quiet behind the scenes not making any noise.

Looking at him you would think he was happy and full of life. However, on the inside, he was wounded and miserable searching for true love. Something he had always valued from his mother was that she shielded him from any harm, showing him nothing but compassion as he was coming up.

Club Palace kept him in sync with the urban scene and somewhat alive as he mingled and endured interesting people day and night. However, it became a challenge for anyone to get close to him, or for him to trust anyone since his trust was broken by his uncle. He had destroyed his life, spirit and pride at an early age.

But even so, he was determined to find the woman of his dreams. Nothing could stop his quest as he carefully observed everyone while examining their motives. He noticed most people when their selfish intentions outshine their best interest from the heart. He had experienced this coming up and was well aware that most would only try and retrieve what they could obtain from him without the sincerity of their heart ever playing a role to obtain it.

Something his auntie instilled in him, and a lesson he would never forget after her death in a car accident, was that honesty and trust is hard to find in people especially when you have something they want. Always watch the motives they present towards you to discern their worth. If you find the central point and motivating force as to why they came to you, most unnecessary heartaches can be foreseen and prevented. Otherwise, they will only bring you down.

Doug had the key to life and the necessary life tools, but he was still missing the lock to fit it. However, possessing the tools is pointless if the ability to put them to use is not connected.

Club Elegant flourished and as things took off he acted as though he was really enjoying the limelight. Besides, no one knew any different and he was more confused than anyone could imagine as flocks of women were constantly throwing themselves at him. He took it all in, casually having flings here and there, hiding behind the mask of the pain he was feeling.

During every altercation, a silent whisper of his worst fear would come out and bring up his past destroying any hope of having a good time. His uncle had become a ghost in his mind, consistently playing with his thoughts, bringing the vaguest memory of what happened to him back in his head every time he became engaged in sexual intercourse with a female. It was now beginning to become too much for Doug to bare. Being a young man fresh out of college trying to find his way, he had to find a way out and cure this problem before it took complete control.

He didn't want to let his desires rule him out, but somehow he knew eventually it would come to the surface. Therefore, he decided to make an appointment to see a therapist and get some professional help before it escalated any further. He had no one that he was close to that he could confide in about his everyday problems, especially the ones that were personal.

"Hello, Dr. Linda Powell's office. May I help you?" the receptionist answered warmly.

"Yes, my name is Doug Walsh."

"How may I help you Mr. Walsh?" she continued.

"I would like to make an appointment to see Dr. Powell."

"Okay, can you hold on while I check her schedule, sir?" she asked politely.

"Yes!" Doug replied .

There was only a brief pause before the woman came back on line."Hello, Mr. Walsh."

"Yes, I'm still here."

"Would 9:00 A.M. Thursday morning work for you, sir?"

"Yes, that's fine."

"Will you be paying cash or by insurance sir?"

"Insurance," Doug replied.

"Thank you. Our rates are posted here, however, I can explain them to you over the phone if you would like," she exclaimed.

"No, thank you. That won't be necessary," Doug shot back.

"Okay, Thursday at 9:00 a.m. I'll see you then, sir," the receptionist stated.

"Thank you very much," Doug said before hanging up the phone.

Doug felt relief knowing he had taken the first step in combating his problem and not procrastinating anymore. Hopefully this would help him gain control of his thoughts and emotions and trust others. He wanted to open up to the possibility of finding what he was searching for.

CHAPTER 1

Douglas Antonio Walsh was born on December 15, 1969 to Douglas and Jackie Walsh, who were enlisted in the United States Army and stationed at Fort Bragg in Fayetteville, North Carolina.

After the birth of their son, Jackie Walsh completed her term and became a full-time mother raising her son using valuable principles she had acquired while in service, while Douglas senior continued to pursue his career as an Army Captain. Life was grand in the southern town, even though it had its share of hardships due to racism during the sixties. But through dedication, determination and hard work they overcame every obstacle that crossed their path and overcame the inevitable to create a somewhat normal life for their family.

Jackie Walsh devoted all of her time raising her son Doug to be well-mannered and respectable in every aspect. Born into the Baptist faith, she encouraged him to treat people with dignity and show kindness to all. Doug followed this concept well and adapted to the ways of his mother's teachings. He spent the majority of his time around her, refusing to even play with the other kids most of the time. He became astonishingly attached to his mom and praising her every command. He was a humble son. Something she took pride in acknowledging was how well-mannered Doug was, and that she had single-handedly raised her son. She wanted him to mingle more with the other kids and do routine activities. Ultimately, she decided to take classes in real estate to become more active since she was bored sitting home daily.

Things took off well, however, Doug thought otherwise, since he was accustomed to seeing his mother daily and taking him to school as well as picking him up at the end of the day. The change had him confused since his mother was unhappy about something that he didn't understand. Eventually, it worked out, and his mother went on and got her real estate license. She landed a job with a real estate firm in the neighboring city of Laurinburg, North Carolina about forty-five minutes away. This interfered with her being a part of Doug's morning routine by having to leave home earlier in time to be at work. So she relied on Doug to uphold his responsibility of preparing himself for school, virtually alone.

His father was now stationed at Fort Meade, in Maryland, which is about three hundred miles away. His tour of duty was scheduled for Vietnam, where he eventually died. In spite of all of the changes that were taking place with his parents, he adapted to the arrangement and continued doing what was expected of him daily.

Now, ten years after the incident with his uncle Sherman and his mother, things somewhat changed again, this time (for the most part) for the worst. He was now in the company of new surroundings, his auntie Ruth and Jerry the son of Sherman his uncle. Jerry turned out to be a bad influence for Doug; because he wasn't raised in the same environment, which excited him, causing Doug to fall right into the trap. Although his auntie still kept him on point, it didn't interfere with their outside activities which was escalating daily.

Upon graduating in 1987 from high school, Doug was street-smart along with his education where he excelled enormously with a 3.5 grade point average. He received a scholarship to North Carolina State University in Raleigh, NC where he soared to new heights quickly. Excited about his prospects, and eager to take on the challenge of being out on his own to create the type of life he had been introduced to by his cousin, was quite overwhelming. He had experienced most things people older than him had yet to see or even thought about doing. He could not wait to put those thoughts to work because he had his dreams to fulfill and create the life he had always wanted for himself.

Upon his first years of college and his 18th birthday, he acquired control of his own finances, which provided him the means to do whatever he wanted. He did not realize corruption was at its peak. He went at everything with a passion, by purchasing a condo and moving out of the dorm at school. Chasing women was his main concept. All women were targeted. He then purchased a brand new 1987 BMW, along with tailor-made suits, and a multitude of stylish clothes to enhance his persona. The change had taken place from the well-mannered kid, into an arrogant and confident conservative young man full of ideas.

Doug had already had his hand in dealings with drugs through his cousin Jerry and now he was able to finance even more which he was eager to do considering he never had to handle any of the product. He thought to himself; why not enhance it since he had access to the money to do so. So he increased his investment and trusted his cousin to handle all the business affairs regarding the sale of the drugs. In time, it became very profitable and helped establish him that much more financially. He decided to invest in other business ventures as he gained ideas from his classes in school where he took up Business Administration. He purchased apartment buildings and renovated them along with a few split-level houses and various other town houses in the city. He was slowly becoming a business magnate with an incredible amount of assets and responsibility to keep things completely organized. He had purchased an office building to handle his real estate affairs and hired staff to run the operation along with an accountant to keep the books in order as he acquired his license.

Optimistic and challenged by his efforts, Doug was on his way and saw no obstacles in his path to prevent him from achieving his goals.

Yet he wasn't completely satisfied because he hadn't obtained all he wanted and was far from being finished. Now in his last year of college and on the edge of graduating, his life took another change for the better this time, at 22 years old or at least that's what he thought anyway. Completing class one morning, he left school at 10:30 a.m. and headed for the office to check on things when he encountered a young woman standing beside a red Corvette which was parked on the side of the road. The hood of the car was up which indicated to him that she was having trouble. He decided to stop and offer his help as he couldn't resist this precious looking individual with her long black hair and curvaceous body. She also had a face that could grace the cover of any magazine. Doug pulled up beside the Corvette and gets out of his BMW. "Excuse me; can I be of any help?" he asked calmly smiling.

"I certainly hope so. I can't seem to find the problem myself. It just cut off all of a sudden," she explained nonchalantly.

"Well to be honest, I'm not much of a mechanic, but if I can give you a ride somewhere I will," Doug replied openly. Hoping she would accept his offer so he could make his move, he decided that was his best option since he had no thoughts of even trying to help get the car started or greasing his hands on it.

"Thank you! That would be nice because I have an appointment to make and I don't want to be late," she said seriously.

"No problem!" Doug replied. "By the way, my name is Doug

Walsh," he responded.

"Hi Doug, I'm Wanda McDonald," she said shyly. Impressed by her demeanor, Doug closed the hood of her Corvette while she retrieved her belongings in the car. He proceeded to open the door for her to store her bags in the back seat and help her in the car before going to the driver's side.

"So Doug, what kind of work do you do?" she asked faintly.

"I'm in my last year of college," Doug said hesitantly.

"College! What are you studying?" she shot back.

"Business Administration amongst various other things," Doug replied grinning.

"What various other things?" she inquired further showing her curiosity.

"Basically, you right now," Doug said smiling.

"Oh, excuse me, sir," she said passionately.

"So do you have obligations to someone?" Doug asked her bluntly.

"Not anyone in particular right now," she answered vaguely.

"Oh, I'm sorry. I've gotten so carried away I haven't even asked you where you need to go, forgive me," Doug replied slowly.

"That's okay; I'm enjoying your conversation. I have an appointment at the beauty salon down on East Crown Street 1400 block."

"Good! That's around the corner from my office," Doug told her. "What office? I thought you were in school," she asked suddenly. "I am in school and I have a real estate business. I established it about three years ago, amongst various other prospects," Doug replied.

"Interesting, you are full of surprises aren't you?" she said faintly.

"Not really, although things are complex at times," Doug admitted.

"So what kind of work do you do Wanda?" Doug asked directly. "Well, you are taking me there now," she told him bluntly.

"So you are a beautician?" Doug said sharply.

"Oh snap, you figured that out on your own Mr. Walsh?" she said jokingly. Seeing the humor she was implying, he decided to play along. He was sensing his progress which was his intention. "I guess you could say that Ms. McDonald," he shot back.

Upon pulling into the parking lot, Doug noticed the shop was closed and thought to himself she was indeed early. "Seems you are not late after all, it has not opened yet," he said.

"That's because I am just arriving," she said with laughter. "I also own the shop, Mr. Walsh," she said in a remote manner.

"Oh! Excuse me, Ms. Thang," Doug implied smartly. Thinking of his next move to satisfy his desire for her knowing she had sparked his interest the minute he set eyes on her.

"Thanks for the ride. I really appreciate it very much, Mr. Walsh. And tell me, how much do I owe you?" she implied softly.

"Oh! There is no charge. However, I would like to see you again if that's alright with you," Doug asked her smiling.

"Sure! I would really enjoy that a lot," she replied back. Totally ecstatic at the thought of the sensational-looking woman accepting his invitation to meet again and give him the chance to increase their friendship. Doug thought to himself about what he could do spectacular to impress her and conquer her heart for he had to have her. He was now feeling as though she was the woman he had been searching for and wasn't about to let her get away. He was determined to make her a part of his stable, yet she somehow seemed to take control of his emotions and that was indeed a first.

"Maybe we can have lunch or dinner soon?" Doug insisted openly.

"That would be nice, whenever you decide," she said softly.

"Are you going to give me your number?" Doug asked.

"Actually, I somehow feel you will know how to contact me when you want to take me out," she implied grimly, knowing if he was really interested she would be seeing him again face to face at the shop without making it easy for him. Besides, she wanted him to show up so her girlfriends could help evaluate her new prospect and the possibilities; something most men have no knowledge of or even realize for that matter. However, Doug was well aware and eager to play her game because little did she know she was his prey and would eventually succumb to his advances to provide for his every need and various others, if need be. When the time arose for it anyway...

CHAPTER 2

Wanda McDonald was a well-raised young woman from a middle class family that frequented church on Sundays. She was 21 years old and fresh out of college who also had her sights set on starting a family and living comfortable in every aspect. Her parents were hard workers and encouraged her to achieve the highest standards in life available to her whenever presented. She instilled this advice in her mind and consistently pursued it all her life; and now that she had seen an opportunity to increase her lifestyle even further, she was not about to let that slip away by any means. After exiting the car, Doug helped retrieve her bags and walked her to the door of the salon. As she opened the door with her key and they stepped inside, Doug was astonished at the sight of the exquisite and large salon that was elegantly furnished. He was overwhelmingly impressed.

"This place is huge and very nice, Wanda," Doug implied honestly. Honored by his remarks and graciously smiling at his comments she responded accordingly.

"Thank you, my parents gave it to me for graduation. It has possibilities," she said politely.

"That it does my dear and some," Doug remarked.

"If you want, you can look around," she inquired, hoping to get him to stick around a little longer.

"Maybe some other time, I need to check up on a few things at the office and make sure things are in order there," he said.

"Okay, well thanks again for the ride," she obliged.

"Oh, you are more than welcome, hopefully I will see you later, maybe even tonight perhaps," Doug inquired nicely.

"Well, I'll be here until 9:00 p.m. if you decide to come," she told him. Disappointed, he couldn't spend more time with her, she gave him that look to enhance the awareness of interest she had for him as Doug acknowledged it, winking his eye.

Little did they know that they both wanted each other equally and they were determined to make it happen. Doug then headed for the door smiling, opened the door and accidentally bumped into a young lady entering as he was exiting. "Excuse me, I'm so sorry," he apologized as her big brown eyes captured his attention wholeheartedly.

"That's alright, I should have been watching where I was going instead of holding my head down," she replied back. Doug continued on, got into his car and proceeded around the corner to his office. The woman entered the salon, impressed and smiling with thoughts running through her mind a mile a minute. "Who was that magnificent specimen that just walked out of here bumping into me at the door?" she asked Wanda.

"Now, why would you ask that Rita?" Wanda implied.

"Because he is fine and I have never seen him before," she said. "Good! Let's keep it that way because he's off limits to you," Wanda shot back angrily knowing how Rita gets down.

"Well, excuse me. No need to get touchy about it. I only asked. It's not like I want him," she remarked smartly. While in her mind, she was already making plans of seeing him again. Rita worked with Wanda renting a booth as were about 10 other women who kept the salon full, constantly gossiping every day; Tuesday through Saturday.

Wanda was well aware of how Rita thought and what she would do as she had experienced her and the other actions for a whole year now. But she couldn't resist asking her opinion of what she thought of Doug.

"So, you like my new man, huh?" she asked Rita in a low tone.

"Girl, the brother is straight. Where you meet him? Does he have any friends?" she asked excitedly, hoping Wanda would respond.

"Now, you are asking too many questions," Wanda replied. "I only wanted your opinion," she said.

Suddenly, the front door came open and a slew of women entered the salon along with most of the women that worked there; renting booths at the same time. All conversation ceased between the two women, as it was time for them to resume business as usual, something Wanda always took seriously and made a top priority. She went about preparing things in order for the materials needed for everyone to do their jobs as usual. Observing Rita, instinctively watching her every move and knowing exactly what thoughts were in her devious mind ,she knew she would have to take precautions the next time Doug came around which was possibly later on that night and she would be ready for the challenge.

Doug entered the office happy and fulfilled, excited about his new found friend. He was greeted by his receptionist Michelle, whom he was intimately involved with; although she was married with two kids of her own. However, he never worried because he knew the relationship would never go any further than regular flings around the office, in which they both were comfortable with .

"Hello Michelle, how was your day?" Doug asked upon entering.

"Fine, I can't complain. How are you Mr. Walsh?" she responded back.

"Did I get any calls this morning?" he asked her.

"Yes! A Mr. Jerry Smith has called numerous times and informed me to have you call him ASAP. He said your cell phone was off and he couldn't contact you this morning," Michelle replied. "All the others are posted on your desk in your office along with a few papers for you to sign before I can send out the memos," she informed him gracefully smiling.

"Thanks, I'll take care of it now," he answered. As he opened his office door, he checked his cell phone and for sure he had forgotten to put it back on after class. He already knew what his cousin wanted, so he would set up their meeting later, after he took care of his business. After making all his calls and signing the papers Michelle left on his desk; he phoned Jerry and told him to meet him for lunch at Applebee's on Maintenance Road in twenty minutes. Doug then informed Michelle on the intercom the papers were ready. She entered, walking seductively towards his desk with a look of lust in her eyes, wearing a tight short skirt and a low cut blouse while looking in his eyes.

"Is there anything else you need Mr. Walsh?" she asked softly. Knowing exactly what she was implying, he stood and said, "Not right now, but I'll need your services when I return later on," he said smiling.

She then eased closer and whispered seductively, "I'll be waiting to supply your every need, sir." As she rubbed her hand slowly up to his crotch and squeezed his manhood. Doug couldn't resist the temptation of the older woman as she knew how to keep him aroused in many ways he had never experienced before with anyone else in his life.

Michelle Robinson was very persistent. "I'll be back around 3:00 after class," he told her.

"What time is your class?" she asked.

"1:30 p.m., I'm going to meet a client for lunch right now. If you need me call my cell phone," he informed her.

"I need you right now," she shot back with a serious look. He grinned and kissed her softly on the cheek before exiting the door. Doug was happy that Michelle was older and married and presented no obligations other than sex, but he didn't understand why a woman of thirty five and that attractive could possibly have so much energy. She had sex three to four times a week with him in the office and who knows how many times at home. He had met her husband, who was somewhat of a jock and showed an intensive amount of love for her around him, at a business meeting.

However, Doug knew something wasn't right and it didn't add up. Yet he didn't waste energy trying to figure it out as long as it didn't interfere with her job or cause any problems, otherwise, it was fine by him. She not only kept him satisfied sexually, she kept things running smoothly and Doug respected her in that aspect, making sure she was comfortable.

She single-handedly ran the office and monitored the three other real estate agents Doug had working there; making sure things were always on point. Michelle had become very valuable to Doug as his personal comforter that kept him somewhat grounded and focused where he was content. However, Doug never expressed this worth to her for fear of taking advantage of her options; therefore, he kept her in the dark and constantly maintained the arrangement as normal to gain her trust. Little did she know she was constantly being tested, as were everyone else that had any dealings or connections with Doug Walsh.

At 12:20 p.m., Doug pulled into the lot of Applebee's and greeted his cousin Jerry, who was waiting in his Mercedes parked near the front with a view of the road that was full of lunch hour traffic. "So, what's been happening cuz?" Jerry asked concerned.

"Same old thing man, taking care of business and hitting the books to finish school," Doug responded.

Jerry reached into his Armani suit and handed Doug an envelope under the table, smiling, "here's your take for this week," he said. "I've been calling you all morning, but I kept getting the answering machine and you know I don't like to leave messages on a machine," he stated with a serious look on his face. "Nevertheless, here's what I wanted to talk to you about that's so important. We're making about

50 grand a week clear a piece, but I just got word some heavy hitters just hit town spreading love like butter and we can increase our profits 2 to 3 percent with the quantity of weight they got. Basically for a small investment we can pull in a cool million within a month, flipping it in the way I have planned using my workers out there. Are you game or what?" Jerry asked, looking into his eyes.

"That all depends on my brother," Doug responded.

"Doug, on what?" Jerry inquired.

"Depends on how much the investment is and how it goes down," Jerry said. "Well, we both be putting up 250 grand a piece and I'm handling the whole transaction with a few of my workers as backup of course. So there's no need to worry because you won't be involved." Jerry assured him.

Doug was hesitant to speak as he thought about the amount of money he had to trust his cousin to handle, yet he really wouldn't be losing anything if something went wrong since he had already made him more than that over the years. "Are you sure you can pull this off?" Doug asked looking intensely serious.

"No problem cuz, trust me. Have I ever let you down?"Jerry asked.

"Okay, when is it going down?" Doug asked.

"Tomorrow, I'll need your half tonight in order for me to put things in motion," Jerry told him.

"Alright, I'll meet you tonight. Come by around 10:00 o'clock. I'm having a friend over for dinner." Doug told him smiling.

"Solid, I'll be there. Is it a female friend?" Jerry implied curiously. "As a matter of fact, it is, cousin," Doug responded.

"Hey, would it be too much for me to bring a female friend," Jerry asked.

"I don't know, I just met this one today and I haven't had a chance to see exactly where she's at or where it's going thus far cuz," Doug replied.

"Isn't that a coincidence, I just met this one last night at the bar," he said.

"And you haven't had time to get to know her either, huh?" Doug replied back.

"Nope!" Jerry shot back.

"Well, bring her over. I'm preparing steaks along with the trimmings and breaking out the crystal. It's on for sure," Doug hollered.

"Thanks man. I didn't know where I was going to take her tonight cause I can't afford to be seen out there with her," Jerry stated sharply.

"Why is that?" Doug inquired concerned.

"Because a player has to keep his game tight," Jerry shot back. "Oh, I thought she was married or something," Doug inquired, concerned.

"Nah, but she's tight enough," he insisted. "Is there anything you want me to bring along?" Jerry asked.

"I'm sure I'm stocked with enough to supply four people with whatever we're going to need tonight," Doug stated firmly.

"Good! I'll see you there at ten o'clock sharp," Jerry said smoothly.

"Sure thing cuz, you going to order?" Doug asked him. They ordered and ate in somewhat of a hurry before they went their separate ways, as Doug had about thirty minutes before his next class started. He took off heading towards the school, planning in his head how he was going to entertain Wanda tonight.

CHAPTER 3

Doug made arrangements for Wanda's car to be towed and fixed while he was finishing the preponderance of thoughts in his head to prepare for the night ahead. After class, he went back to the office, and finished his fling with Michelle and gathered his notes after completing his return calls for the day and closing up.

"Thanks Mr. Walsh; that was really nice," Michelle commented, leaving Doug smiling as she took strides towards her car; thinking how lovely and charming she was; noticing how her ass bounced, with every step enhancing her unique body for a woman of her age. He then headed around the corner to the salon to retrieve the car keys to the Corvette.

Upon arriving, he noticed the parking lot was full of cars which showed she had an incredible amount of customers. He then proceeded inside to see women galore as everyone suddenly froze at his presence as though he was from another planet. Looking around for Wanda, who was nowhere in sight, he was approached by an attractive woman with braids. "May I help you?" she asked politely smiling.

"I'm looking for Ms. Wanda McDonald," Doug said slowly.

"Oh, she's in her office in the back right down that hall. Is she expecting you?" The woman asked directly.

"No, but I would like to surprise her," Doug requested. He headed down the hall. As he approached the office, he noticed the door partially open and peeked inside where he noticed her using the computer, looking exquisitely beautiful.

Doug tapped on the door and stepped inside. "Hello beautiful," he expressed charmingly.

Showing admiration toward the figure standing before her, "Hi Doug. I didn't expect to see you so soon," Wanda stated softly. However, she was more than happy that he was there cause he had been on her mind all day. She then clicked off her computer where she had already punched him up and was reviewing his assets at the moment that he walked in.

"I came by to retrieve your car keys," he said.

"Excuse me?" she shot back firmly. "I've had your car towed and fixed this morning," he told her.

"Well, thank you. You're such a gentleman," she said happily. Thinking to herself, she knew her instincts were right about him and couldn't wait to find out more about this interesting young man. Little did she know that was his sentiments exactly. Upon passing him her car keys, she gestured toward finding a way to leave with him. "How are you going to drive both cars?" she inquired seductively while looking into his eyes.

Seeing his chance to spend more time with her he stated smoothly. "Can you leave right now?"

"Sure!" She shot back hurriedly. She grabbed her purse and informed one of the girls to take over. As she and Doug was exiting the salon, they attracted the attention of her patrons while hearing some mumbles about the attractive gentleman's presence. Doug held the door open escorting Wanda into the passenger side of the car and gently closing the door as he proceeded to the other side. Upon leaving the parking lot, they engaged in a conversation.

"That's very considerate of you, having my car fixed," she stated softly.

"It's the least I could do for an attractive lady as you," Doug said smoothly, knowing it was time to compliment her and reveal his feelings to her.

"Thank you Mr. charming," she said slyly.

"Oh, you're quite welcome and deserving of the compliment," he stated.

"You're quite interesting yourself Doug. Are you married or single? If that's not being too personal and you don't mind my asking," she stated firmly.

"I'm single and all alone and 'No' I don't mind," he said smiling. "How about you? Are you single?" he inquired.

"Unfortunately, yes, I'm single," she said grinning.

"Well, it seems we have a lot in common, therefore, I feel we should explore the possibilities presented before us; what do you think?" Doug asked.

"Sounds like a plan," she said seductively.

"One I'm sure we can put together and accomplish," Doug shot back.

"Well, I never argue with perfection, do you Mr. Walsh?" she said firmly.

"So how does dinner at my place sound tonight?" Doug responded.

"Simply marvelous Doug," she stated with interest. I'll finish up at 7:00 p.m."

"Good! I'll pick you up at 9:00 p.m. Give me your address," he asked her.

She wrote it down on her business card and handed it to him as they approached the dealership where he had her car towed. He then went in while she sat in the car. Curiosity setting in, she decided to lift the console and discovered a 9mm and a new stack of 100 dollar bills sitting between the seats along with a variety of pictures of Doug with some attractive woman, etc. She now knew she had competition and her work was cut out for her in order to have him all to herself because he was a keeper.

Doug exited the dealership after paying for the services on the car and informed Wanda that the fuel injectors were clogged up and should only use premium gas from now on to avoid any problems. He then explained what he planned tonight, letting her know that they would have additional company over with them. He revealed that his cousin would be joining them with a friend that he incidentally hadn't met before; and if that was alright with her, hoping it didn't create a problem. She agreed and told him that it was okay with her. However, she wasn't the least bit comfortable with the idea because she had her own plans and now feared that they would interfere with what she had intended on doing tonight.

Hopefully, she could still somehow work her magic around them because it was definitely going to be a long night to remember. "Take care; I'll see you later tonight," she said while getting into the car. Doug closed her door and smiled before commenting. "Okay, I'm looking forward to it. See you then beautiful,"

Doug followed behind the Corvette as they exited the lot when suddenly his cell phone rang. "Hello!" He answered sharply.

"Hi, Doug," the voice responded.

"Oh! Hi Auntie, how're you doing? I haven't heard from you in a while. What you been up to? Is everything alright?" Doug asked.

"Why yes! I called to let you know that I received a few foreclosures on some properties you might be interested in, being that they have potential," she expressed interest.

Doug knew she always had his best interest at heart and she was one of the few people that he could honestly trust that wasn't out to get his money or scheme in any way for selfish gains. Plus, she was the reason he decided to invest in real estate. She had all the experience and connections. Now he was really curious to hear what she had in store because she always got property that was profitable to the company where he could expand his business.

"Hey! Because it's property, there is two office buildings and a night club for sale that they're auctioning off tomorrow," she said firmly. "However, I'm not really sure the nightclub will be a good investment because it would probably be more trouble than it's worth. But it will be a cheap investment for someone willing to run it properly. By no means am I suggesting you attempt such a feat because I honestly don't think you're up for the task," she concluded.

"Now, the office buildings are a top priority because of their location near downtown, which shouldn't be a problem as far as tenants are concerned," she expressed firmly. "So, what you think Doug?" she asked him.

"Sounds good, both aspects," he informed her to her surprise. "Did I just hear you right?" she shot back angrily.

"Sure! I like them both," Doug responded. "Make it happen for me."

"Are you certain this is what you want?" she asked seriously.

"Yes, ma'am, Auntie. I'm sure," Doug stated firmly. "Ok, make it happen Auntie. I'm counting on you," Doug told her, knowing she could handle all the details and all he would have to do was sign the papers and make the transaction with the bank which created little effort and less work for him to have to deal with.

"I'll call you tomorrow with the details," she told Doug.

"Alright, thanks auntie. I'll take care of you," Doug insisted. He knew she would receive a large percentage as the commission for selling the property as she acquired it with his money. She knew her business well and taught Doug the tricks of the trade.

"No problem, talk to you later," she stated before hanging up. Doug thought to himself another $300,000 dollar investment would really boost his assets in the years to come and generate even more clientele, which is what he went in the business for. It also presented a front for him to launder the money he had generated from drugs which he couldn't leave in the safe forever. Besides, he had a good accountant to work it out for him and handle the books to shield him from any tax evasion. Once he arrived home and prepared everything for the night's festivities, Doug got showered and dressed in time to pick up Wanda while putting on his best impression yet.

He took pride in doing this with all the women he had encountered in an effort to find his most pivotal prize. Once he found her house, he was amused at the split level as it was similar to a few he owned. He approached the door and rang the bell. To his surprise, he was greeted by a graceful looking middle age woman around fifty.

"Hello, my name is Doug. I am here to pick up Wanda," Doug said politely.

"Hi, how are you doing? She's expecting you. I'm Wandas' mother, Carolina, do come in," she said pleasantly opening the door for Doug. Shocked by the surprise that she was staying with her parents, Doug sensed opportunities arises in numbers and conditions. "Won't you have a seat?" The woman inquired softly. "Wanda's coming down."

"Thank you," Doug responded.

Impressed, he looked around the immaculately clean house that had been furnished with elegant looking furniture and remarkable paintings that adorned the walls. Wanda had something to do with the decorations. She approached the stairwell as Doug looked up and almost fell out his seat at the sight of this luscious black beauty showing her beautiful body in a matching skin tight skirt and pumps which left him speechless. He was stuck on her like glue, unaware of her amazement. Wanda kept her eyes seductively locked with his in a way that drove Doug crazy.

"I see you are prompt, Mr. Walsh. I like that in a man," she said softly.

"I never keep a woman waiting," he stated briefly.

"I appreciate and agree with that concept," she expressed in a low tone. "I see you have met my mother?" she asked him.

"Yes, very pleasant lady. I see where you get yours," he smiled. "Why thank you Doug," her mother expressed. "Maybe now she'll pay more attention to those attributes of mine that she displays all the time."

"She only said that because everyone says I'm more like my father," she told him firmly. Winking her eyes and laughing at her mother. "Hopefully you'll meet my father and see for yourself later, he's out of town right now on business," Wanda explained. "I'm ready if you are Doug," she told him.

"Well, it's nice to meet you Mrs. McDonald, I look forward to it again where we have more time," Doug politely stated smiling.

"Alright, I'd like that; you all have fun and be careful" she said happily.

"We will mom, don't wait up," she told her mother. As they drove along the highway, Doug couldn't resist picking her mind, testing her mentality.

"So, Wanda now that you are established in business where do you see yourself in about five years?" Doug asked in a serious tone.

"Married with children, a nice comfortable home, happy as far as I can possibly go into every aspect of my life, Mr. Walsh," she said with a serious look that meant business in every sense of the word. Doug was now sure he'd ran into the woman of his dreams as she had now answered his question with ease and said exactly what he wanted to hear; just as if she actually read his mind with his exact detail of expectation.

The moment they pulled onto the road leading to his house silence gripped the air. As Wanda looked in amazement at the tall beams in front and the massive size structure, she became immediately overwhelmed as she couldn't believe her eyes.

"Doug, is this your house?" she asked frantically.

"Yes!" Doug responded.

"And you stay here alone?" she inquired curiously.

"Of course!" He shot back noticing admiration all over her face. Doug knew when he purchased this Mediterranean masterpiece made of stone and marble with 8,968 square feet of interior and the elusive infinity pool- this five bath, 2 and a half bath, five bedroom estate was unique to serve the purpose for the family he wanted and was indeed an attention grabber- the minute he walked into it. And now was the time to showcase his talent and ability to impress the woman he wanted there with him for life. He couldn't wait to show her the gourmet kitchen and marble fireplace in the massive size living room with its marble floors, along with the beautiful patio overlooking the exquisitely extraordinary twin waterfall in the back. It was all a woman could ask for, amongst various other things, that he was ready and willing to supply.

Upon reaching the house, Doug retrieved the remote and pushed the button to the garage door. As the garage door rose, he drove inside and brought the BMW to a halt. The garage contained a Mercedes, a completely restored 69 Camaro and motorcycle. Wanda was equally impressed as they all looked new.

"I take all these are yours also?" she stated cleverly.

"I consider these my toys; would you like to play with some of them?" Doug asked with a grin.

"Wouldn't that be nice and a far cry from my Corvette," she said. Doug was elated that half his plan was accomplished and was ready to complete the rest. As they entered the house from the side corridor, the hallway was adorned with elegant black Nubian art and dimly lit lights above leading into the massive living room where Doug picked up a remote and at the flick of a button the fireplace lit up beaming its light across the elegantly styled room.

Music blared, giving the sensation of a unique ensemble of jazz as if they were in a club. Wanda was highly amazed at the sight of the room and all of its accessories. "Doug, this is a magnificent house," she expressed excitedly.

"Thanks, but you haven't seen your hive yet," Doug shot back.

"What do you mean by that?" she responded curiously smiling.

"I'm sure you will figure it out in time," Doug stated slowly. "Can I get you something to drink?" he asked politely.

"That would be nice. Do you have any orange juice?" she inquired. At that moment, she took Doug totally by surprise to where he went into a state of shock and froze thinking back on his unpleasant disgraceful childhood. Something he didn't like to revisit anytime. Noticing Doug just standing there as if he had seen a ghost, Wanda wondered if something had happened.

"Doug, are you alright? You look like you seen a ghost."

"Sure, I'm alright. It's just that; nothing," he mumbled softly. "I'm sorry, but I never drink orange juice. I'm allergic to it and I break out. Anything else you care to drink?" he asked her nicely.

"Well, what do you have?" she shot back.

"Let's go see," he said as they walked to the gourmet kitchen. Wanda couldn't help expressing her thoughts of the beautiful setting before her.

"Oh my goodness, this is beautiful. I would love to have a kitchen like this Doug," she said in a serious tone.

"Really?" Doug responded. "Well, it wouldn't hurt to have someone to share this with," Doug said smiling.

"Be careful, Mr. Walsh. I may never leave," she said winking.

"Well, you do have a point, because a man's got to know his limitations," Doug responded cleverly while looking in her eyes.

"That's right, because a girl could get used to this real easy and become attached quickly," Wanda implied grinning.

After fixing glasses of coke they then toured the rest of the massive estate. Wanda expressed admiration in every room she entered, overwhelmingly ecstatic at the sight while thinking about how she would fit in so well there, and knowing that was part of her plan. However, she had no idea he was established to this extent. But that only increased her desire to capture his heart and live comfortably through his support.

Doug was thrilled that things were going as he planned and had no idea it would actually be so easy to convince her in this manner. Being that she wasn't presenting much of a challenge against his advances which was fine, he didn't want to waste too much energy enticing her anyway. Now after dinner, his next move was to become intimate. He thought this might be the challenge he was looking for being that she had class and showed potential in areas most didn't.

Suddenly the doorbell rang and Doug looked at his Rolex, 9:58 p.m. Jerry was right on time as they went downstairs. "There's our guest," he told her as she sat in the living room. Doug headed down the corridor and answered the door, shocked at the sight of the lovely young lady standing beside his cousin. "What's up cuz? Come on in," Doug insisted.

"What's happening man? This is my friend Rita. Rita this is Doug," Jerry said introducing them.

"Yes! We met briefly in passing," Doug stated. "How you doing?"

"Fine. I had no idea you were going to be the host. What a coincidence, we meet again," Rita said instinctively clever.

"Well, come on in the living room. Wanda is waiting for us there," Doug said.

Rita knew right then that Wanda would be surprised and unhappy to see her there, but she could care less right now. The minute they

U. E. Wynn

entered the living room, Wanda noticed Rita and couldn't imagine how she ran into Doug's cousin. Knowing how she operated, it wasn't going to be a pleasant night. She wasn't too fond of the woman who worked in her shop, but she tolerated her anyway (unaware they were half-sisters). However, she wasn't about to let her destroy what she had in store for her and Doug under the circumstances.

"Jerry, this is Wanda. Wanda, my cousin Jerry and you two already know one another," Doug said, speaking to Rita.

"Hello Jerry! I'm glad to meet you," Wanda responded.

"Hi! How bout yourself?" he shot back. "So you already know Rita huh?" Jerry asked nonchalantly.

"Yes! She rents a booth in my salon," Wanda answered.

"Something smells like Cajun," Rita remarked.

"Yes, that's the steaks. Wanda will you help me?" Doug asked.

"Sure!" She replied, following him to the kitchen.

"Wanda, I sense tension in the air. What's up?" Doug asked her.

"That's cause she is a snake, Doug," Wanda responded.

"Then why does she work around you?" Doug asked.

"As a favor to a friend, I rented her the booth, only to discover later it was a mistake," she expressed seriously. "Hopefully she won't be there much longer, as she plans to find her own shop which can't seem to be soon enough."

"I take it you don't care too much for her," Doug replied.

"Bingo! I don't trust her," she said angrily.

After setting the table and finishing their meal, Doug and Jerry went into the living room, while Wanda voluntarily chose to clean up and insisted that Rita help her. She knew what she was capable of and so she had to set her straight right away. However, Rita was more than eager for the chance to express what she was feeling much to Wanda's surprise.

"Girl, this crib is nice. I could do some things in here and be set for life," she expressed excitedly.

"Don't even think about it witch. I know how you get down, so stop entertaining the damn thought. It ain't happening," Wanda shot back furiously.

"Don't hate, I got to get mines," she said smartly.

"Well, it's nothing here for you Ms. Thang," Wanda said angrily.

"That's funny. I don't see a ring on that brother's finger," she

32

implied.

"But you will discover one around your eye if you step out of line tonight. This ain't no game and I ain't playing," Wanda said seriously.

"What's wrong? You scared of a little competition?" Rita implied.

"If you flatter yourself," Wanda said laughing.

"Well, let's see about that," Rita said looking grim.

"Alright, I warned you. Don't take it for granted. I meant what I said and I will get ghetto on your ass in here," she said promptly.

"So it's like that? I thought we were girls," Rita said firmly.

"Whatever gave you that impression? You're highly mistaken and couldn't be further from the truth," Wanda stated harshly.

"Thanks for showing your true colors. I hope you recognize it when you see them again," Rita said angrily.

"Is that a threat?" Wanda asked straight faced.

"Not at all, it's a damn fact, my dear," Rita shot back as she headed towards the living room with Wanda behind her.

They all gathered together snugly drinking Hennessy and talking while the smooth sound of Gil Scott Heron played lightly through the room. As tension flowed through the entire time, Jerry sensing something wrong tried breaking the ice by telling a corny joke but to no avail. So he decided it was time to leave.

"Hey cuz, I got a surprise for you. Don't mess it up," Doug said seriously.

He then walked upstairs and retrieved one of his Armani suits that he had put two hundred and fifty grand inside and brought it down, handing it to Jerry giving him the look that only they knew.

"This is for the grand opening Thanksgiving night cuz," he told him.

"What grand opening?" Jerry inquired curiously.

"The grand opening of my new night club," Doug responded sharply. "I'm acquiring it tomorrow, hopefully, if things work out, which I'm sure they will cause I have a good realtor working on it," he said smiling.

"And who might that be, as if I don't already know?" Jerry shot back.

"That's right, you know her very well," Doug stated. Both women were curious as to who they were referring to as Wanda started thinking about the woman she had seen in the pictures with Doug inside his car at the dealership. However, they stayed in suspense as they never revealed the source. Jerry said his goodbyes and proceeded towards the door as Rita followed with a chip on her shoulder saying nothing. After escorting them out, Doug walked slowly back into the living room looking into the eyes of Wanda.

"Are you alright, beautiful?" he implied.

Hesitant, she answered. "Yes! I'm glad they're gone. She's really a pain," she told Doug.

"Obviously she's not your friend," Doug stated vaguely.

"No, she isn't, besides I only have acquaintances. There are very few I trust enough to call a friend. I'm mostly a loner," she told him.

"So how do you maintain?" Doug asked concerned.

"I understand the concept of how time heals the heart and my faith provides for me to do the rest," she said positively.

"But how does that provide for your motives?" Doug stated sharply.

"Actually, it doesn't, it keeps me grounded and focused to see reality as it unfolds; because my life is an everyday struggle. So I'm optimistic and I realize I have the courage to change things around me. In order to create happiness," she said from within. "So that's your main objective? Happiness?" Doug asked sharply. "Basically, all I want is to find someone to love, that loves me and knows he's totally mine," she said sincerely.

"That's possible and within your reach," Doug told her boldly. "And I'm determined to achieve my dream," she expressed smiling.

"I really admire those attributes in you, a woman who depicts the odds and strives for what she wants in life," Doug replied back.

"Darling, that's the only way you are going to obtain it; ask for it." "Wanda I want you to become a part of my life. Is that how it's done?" Doug inquired frankly.

Smiling at his approach, she said softly, "Yes! I'd be honored." Doug took her hand, led her to the bedroom and they made passionate love all night long and parted ways that morning. Their relationship was now open for possibilities; leaving them prone to whatever transpired now and eager for the chance to become productive together. Both were satisfied with the evening and looked forward to the days that were to follow.

Behind The Mask

CHAPTER 4

The year was now 1990 and Doug was prosperous in every aspect of his life. Things were going well. He had started a successful business (real estate) and obtained a glamorous nightclub. Found several relationships with some very interesting women and acquired more financially than he actually needed in a lifetime. Life was grand. The month of November of that year was planned to be memorable as he set the stage for his grand opening. Doug always took pride in the events. That was his way of creating loads of happiness amongst people, to discover their true character and manipulate from within something he'd mastered, or so he thought.

Thanksgiving night would be a feast to remember as he planned to open the doors and present the event free of charge. Money wasn't an option and wasn't needed for anything. He knew the idea would attract and establish a clientele.

Doug's plan worked remarkably. There was a house full of distinguished people who gathered to enjoy the free festivities while mingling with the crowd. Being the host had its benefits in many ways as he captured everyone's attention. And this landed him a job as the host of a local hip hop video show. His popularity soared to new heights as he basked in the glory of his new found friends whom he found interesting in their own right. He met loads of interesting people that were in some ways complex, confusing, peculiar, demanding and outspoken amongst various other things.

During was having a conversation with his DJ and good friend Mike, and was complimenting him on his new marriage. He was indirectly getting pointers and looking forward to his own one day, when a sexy young fair skinned lady approached them at the booth.

"Excuse me," she said softly. "Do you have something in there to slow the mood down?"

Doug noticed how easy on the eyes she was and introduced himself and informed her that Mike would be out of service. He insisted that she allow him the first dance and she agreed. As they were dancing, Doug picked her mind finding out all he possibly could about this young stallion.

"Hello, my name is Doug Walsh. I like formal introductions, up close and personal. I hope you don't mind," Doug expressed. The young lady, somewhat amused at his approach, slowly danced as she collected her thoughts before answering.

"No, I don't mind. My name is Yvonne," she said softly.

"So Yvonne, are you having a good time at my opening?" Doug asked.

"Why yes. I didn't know this was your club," she stated.

Doug then stopped and moved towards the booth and introduced her to his DJ Mike as they engaged in conversation, giving each individual insight about one another and providing a foundation for a platonic friendship to develop. He became increasingly interested as the young woman spoke, revealing personal sides of herself, leading him to find her that much more attractive and appealing. Then all of a sudden, he learned that she's engaged and the alarm bells rang as he knew he now had a challenge before him, which he was eager and willing to consider being that she really fascinated him. They continued conversing and passing time when suddenly an exquisite looking female spoke.

"Girl, I'm not a night person, you know that," Yvonne responded.

Smiling widely, the young lady came back. "I know. So how've you been doing?" she asked eagerly.

"Alright! Sorry Cassandra, this is Doug, the host of tonight's events. Doug, this is my friend Cassandra and this is his good friend Mike the DJ," Yvonne replied coyly.

They all spoke in accordance and continued in conversation as Doug forced his undivided attention on Cassandra; she was magnificent in every sense of the word and left him absolutely stunned.

Yvonne noticed the attraction instantly and engaged in conversation with Mike while they conversed, eagerly awaiting the outcome. However, Doug was so overwhelmed he took Cassandra to a table and sat down to discover her every move. Only to find out later on that she was married. Doug was persistent as he had to have the woman sitting before him by all means. The very next morning on November 25th, Cassandra went out early to shop, determined to catch the Christmas sales and garnish what she could before the crowds came, when she heard a voice from a distance. "Girl, I know you enjoyed last night." Cassandra catching Yvonne's voice was shocked to see her in the mall that early.

She turned and faced her smiling widely. "I must say it was nice girl," she shot back candidly. Yvonne was eager to hear what Cassandra and Doug discussed and bled Cassandra from start to finish. However, Cassandra wasn't comfortable discussing another man and she desperately wanted to keep it on the down low. Although she had started seeing signs of her husband having an affair, she kept her faith and hope alive in her marriage. But she couldn't deny that the night before provided comfort for her. And Doug made an incredible impact on her; revamping her confidence and giving her a sense of dignity that she never felt before.

"Are you going to see him again" Yvonne asked curiously.

"I think not!" Cassandra replied quickly.

"Why not?" Yvonne asked.

"Because I am married," Cassandra shot back.

"Then where was your husband last night?" Yvonne stated smartly.

"That's a good question," Cassandra said lightly. Considering the fact that she had no idea where he could have been on Thanksgiving night.

In time, he was convincing and eventually found the passageway into her heart. Little did he know it would become his greatest challenge as she was madly in love with her husband. Although his timing was great as her marriage had started losing its spark after three years, it was to no avail. She wasn't going to be detached.

Cassandra was a very attractive school teacher who fell in love with her high school sweetheart. The only man she ever made love to or encountered in a relationship. Before the night ended they were well acquainted, laughing and inspiring one another to great lengths.

Cassandra introduced Doug to her sister Alicia, a lab technician at a local hospital who was three years her junior who Doug discerned was openly arrogant from her conversation as she joined them. Nevertheless, she had potential in her own way. So far the night was a high success. Presenting Doug with enormous opportunities to prosper in many ways and taking advantage of everyone. He was pleased with his efforts and very much satisfied with their results. However, the one woman that captured his interest eluded him and he couldn't gain as much progress as he wanted with her. But he was determined to pursue her until he succeeded; only time would tell and he knew he had plenty of patience for someone of that caliber.

In case Wanda didn't work out, he now had back up.

"Girl, enjoy it and let it flow freely," Yvonne said frankly. "If it made you feel good, it can't be that bad," she expressed further, hoping Cassandra took advantage of her options.

"I never had a man say those things to me before and remain constantly on my mind," Cassandra stated openly, going against her better judgment expressing her feelings toward the man she just met, the night before.

"Sounds like a plan to me, what things?" Yvonne asked, concealing the fact that she had already overheard their conversation and knew basically every detail.

Cassandra explained partially, before they departed their separate ways, gathered her thoughts and continued shopping.

Meanwhile, Doug made his way over to the townhouse he had now set Wanda up in. Now, away from her mother's house, he was ready to spend quality time with her alone as he did with every woman he was frolickingwith. He made his rounds equal to avoid any suspicion as to his whereabouts at any time and covered his trail with his many business ventures as an excuse for questions of that nature. However, most of the women were in compliance, with no exception, concerning the arrangement and settled for whatever time they could garnish from him. Although they had hopes of one day pinning him down if their marriage every soured (unknown to him).

Doug made passionate love to Wanda all that morning and poured all he had into her vigorously for a couple of hours because he knew he had to make a dramatic impact. However, there was no exception when it came to Wanda because he had a desire for her that he couldn't deny. After pleasing her, they discussed what accessories they were going to put into the townhouse and made arrangements before departing. Doug then headed for the estate, constantly thinking about Cassandra and his desire for her, wondering if he would ever see her again.

Dismissing the thought, he picked up his cell phone and called Jerry, receiving no answer. Growing concerned and wondering whether the transaction went sour, Doug pondered about the fact that he never had to worry about him before. He also realized that he had not heard from him earlier, although he should have heard from him by now. Once he settled in at home, he decided to call his auntie thinking she may know of Jerry's whereabouts, only to find out she had not seen him in over a week. Doug became weary and even more concerned, knowing this was odd behavior for his cousin, who always kept in contact with his mother daily. Doug then called Wanda and asked if she seen Rita lately. She responded by saying she had been coming to work as usual, but acting strangely towards her. He then asked Wanda for Rita's phone number explaining he hadn't seen or heard from his cousin since that night. After receiving Rita's phone number from Wanda, Doug dialed the digits contemplating how he was going to come off on Rita to find out what he needed to know. He decided casually was his best option.

"Hello," the voice murmured softly.

"Hello Rita, this is Doug, Jerry's cousin," Doug explained.

"I know who you are. Hi, so what did I do to deserve this call, can I help you?" she expressed delightfully.

"I was wondering if you've seen my cousin Jerry? I have not heard from him since Monday night when ya'll left my house," Doug explained rationally.

"No, after we left, he dropped me off claiming he had some personal business to tend to," she said why would she respond sarcastically?sarcastically.

"He never mentioned anything else?" Doug asked curiously.

"Well, he did, but it's not something you want to talk about over the phone," she said suddenly.

"We can do lunch," Doug suggested.

"That's no good; I could come over right now," she said coyly.

"Good, you remember how to get here?" Doug asked.

"Sure!" She expressed proudly. "I'm on my way."

Rita now had other plans she wanted to put in motion. And now it was presented to her openly. She dialed her phone quickly as the phone rings. She heard a heavy voice on the other end answer.

"Talk."

"Redbone, I need to holler at you, it's serious. I just got word and we need to discuss it," she said in a serious tone.

"I'll meet you tonight, same place and time," he responded.

"Alright!" She shot back quickly.

"Handle your business," he said and hung up.

Rita hurried and got ready, set her alarm and headed toward the door as she made her way to Doug's estate. She contemplated about how she planned to approach him.

As she got to the entrance of the estate, her plan was set in place. Hopefully, she would have no interruptions to disrupt her from completing the task. Once she reached the house, Doug met her and invited her in. He wasted no time asking about Jerry.

"He told me that he had a big deal going down, and that I wouldn't be involved. So he was going to meet his crew and take care of it," she replied concerned.

"That's not like him. He always let me know what's going on," Doug told her.

"Did you contact the police?" she asked curiously.

"No, I don't want them involved," Doug said frankly.

"Why not?" Rita asked hectically.

"He may show up later, I'll have someone look for him first," Doug stated sharply.

"Doug, can a lady get a drink?" Rita asked softly.

"I'm sorry, excuse me, where's my manners? I was so hung up talking about my cousin." Doug said apologetically.

"I understand," Rita replied. As Doug prepared the drink, Rita took off her coat revealing her lovely bodacious body with her luscious lips gleaming brightly. She knew Doug would melt once her assets were shown to entice his desire that much more. When he returned with the drinks, she noticed his eyes widen at the sight of her sitting with her legs crossed. Her plan was working and she knew it.

Doug set the drinks on coasters and took his seat beside her as if everything was normal. However, he was in shock as she looked seductively in his eyes.

"I know this is a complex time for you, but maybe you need to relax and I don't want to sound forward, but the timing couldn't be better," she said softly with her eyes roaming.

Doug was beside himself as he couldn't believe his ears. He had been thinking about how he was going to approach her and now she's made it easy. He took her by the hand and led her to the master bedroom. When they entered the room, Rita wasted no time in her quest to seduce him. As she dropped her skirt and unbuttoned her blouse, Doug was glued to the sight of her smooth brown skin. While undoing her bra and panties, she moved toward Doug; unbuttoned his shirt and removed it slowly while kissing him on the lips. She undid his belt and removed his trousers down to his shoes and slung the pants towards the floor in the same motion.

She rubbed her hands from the top of his feet, up his legs and along his thighs gently until she reached his chest. With gentle light kisses, she teased his nipples, rubbing her tongue in circular motions rising up his neck and rubbed her hand down to his manhood. As she slid down and took him whole into her mouth, she gently stroked the length of it vigorously while massaging his testicles and sucking intensely.

Suddenly, footsteps crept toward the door as Rita had her fill of Doug deep in her mouth. Standing in awe of the sight, they walked away gently. Rita then rose above Doug slowly and slid down the length of his manhood with a loud gasp. Gently riding him until she adjusted, then vigorously, she increased her motion, moaning loudly as she reached orgasm. She collapsed beside him drained from the intensity of the enormous climax she had intentionally induced between them in a matter of minutes. After conversing, they showered together and departed after making plans to meet again and remain discreet in agreement.

CHAPTER 5

Doug carried on with his normal daily routine hoping he would soon hear from his cousin and find out what was happening. As he was sitting in his office, the phone rings, "Mr. Walsh, you have a call on line one," Michelle told him.

"Hello!" He answered.

"Doug, I was informed by the police that they found who they think may be Jerry in the park, with a bullet in his head and they've asked me to come verify the body. I'm on my way there now. Do you have any idea what happened?" His auntie asked frantically.

"No! But I plan on finding out," Doug responded instinctively.

"Well, I'm on my way there now," she told him.

"Okay," do you want me to come along?" Doug asked.

"I'll handle it; just see what you can find out," she told him.

Doug knew his auntie was strong, but he didn't expect her to handle it well. However, his work was not cut out for him and he wasn't about to take this lying down.

Doug called one of his cousin's friends and told him what was going on, hoping to get some kind of information out of him. He knew that Leroy did most of his street transactions. However, he had not heard or seen Jerry either. He informed Doug that he was wondering why he had not been around to collect this week's take of the money. Doug informed him to keep it business as usual because he now ran the show and he should only answer to him. They agreed and hung up.

Doug then hired a private investigator and explained the whole ordeal on a client-attorney basis. He lead him in the right direction to find his cousin's killer and told him money was not an option in this matter. So that he would be assured of his undivided attention on the case. Meanwhile, Michelle had been listening to the conversations on the phone as she did with all of his calls, counting his every move to stay abreast of his activities. She then walked into the office and approached Doug slowly.

"Is everything alright Mr. Walsh?" she asked concerned.

"Nothing I can't handle," he replied speedily.

Unaware that she already knew, he revealed what had happened and was shocked at her reply. "I have some people who can take care of those types of things," she expressed seriously.

"In what way?" Doug asked interested.

"Once they find out who did it, the person becomes missing. Anyway, they owe me a favor," she exclaimed.

Doug was hesitant to respond as he now wondered about the kind of woman he was involved with. Because she now had cards she wasn't showing and who knows what she's capable of. However, it not only interested him, it was also very convenient being that he wanted whoever responsible to pay for what they had done. Therefore, he agreed and asked who this individual was in order to check his credentials, as he was hesitant in dealing with someone unknown to him. Michelle explained that he was her cousin and specialized in what's going down in the streets. She then told Doug his name was Carlos Black, A.K.A. Redbone and that she would set up a meeting tonight providing she could actually be there. Doug eyes widened as he knew what she was up to, yet he agreed to her options and set a time he would be home. He then put things in order and proceeded out the door, heading to his class.

While driving along pondering his thoughts, listening to some smooth jazz blaring from his car stereo, he noticed a blue Firebird following him from a distance. To make sure, he intentionally went out of the way to see if it continued in pursuit. His assumption was right. He then pulled over after making a right turn when suddenly the car made a quick U-turn heading in the opposite direction unable to get a glimpse of the driver. Doug wondered in suspense of who it could've been. Dismissing the thought, he continued on to school and completed classes for the day.

Later on that night he met up with Michelle and her cousin Redbone to discuss the details of Jerry's death. As they finished, Doug felt somewhat in awe as he sensed that Redbone acted peculiar as they talked. Nevertheless, they all went their separate ways. Doug headed over to see Wanda and while en route, his phone rang. Auntie Ruth informed him that she confirmed the body to be Jerry and the police think the motive was robbery. After hearing the news, he told her he would be in touch and that he had somebody on the case. Upon arriving at her townhouse, he noticed the lights cut off. He then went to the door and let himself in, hearing the sound of soft music.

He made his way to the bedroom to find Wanda laying there in her underwear, eating ice cream, and watching television. Her shock upon seeing him soon turned into elation.

"Hey handsome," she said smiling.

"How're you doing baby?" Doug shot back.

"I missed you last night, where were you?" Wanda replied.

"Out of town on business," Doug answered. He headed for the shower and Wanda joined him soon after. They made passionate love in and out of the shower all night long. That morning as Doug prepared for the day ahead, he kissed Wanda goodbye. While driving his cell phone rang.

"Hello!" He answered.

"Hi baby, will I see you today?" The voice asked.

Doug was hesitant with his reply since he could not place the owner of the voice. "That depends," he responded.

"On what?" The voice shot back.

"On whether it would be worth it or not," he replied. Suddenly he recognized the voice and knew what she wanted after their last meeting, yet he had no idea Rita would respond so quickly. However, he was ready for the challenge as he enjoyed her just as much. After conversing and making plans he hung up and pulled into the office parking lot. As he entered the building, he noticed a few patrons before heading into his office. A call from his auntie was posted on his desk.

He set his cell phone on his desk and used the office phone to call her back. After the conversation, he left for his class which was a part of his normal routine. During the end of class, he noticed that he left his phone and headed back to the office to retrieve it. Once inside his office, he checked his calls. Michelle entered the office with papers needing his signature. Doug quickly signed the papers with complete trust never noticing the documents.

Suddenly someone enters the office and heard the sound of sex. Unaware of the presence, Doug continued to excite Michelle enormously as she reaches orgasm. As Michelle regained her composure, she exited the office only to be shocked by a middle aged woman sitting there and starring in awe. Realizing she overheard her and Doug as they engaged, she quickly asked the woman if she could assist her.

"I'm here to see Mr. Doug Walsh. My name is Carolina McDonald," the lady replied gently.

"One moment please," Michelle said nicely. Embarrassed and somewhat ashamed that the woman overheard their coupling, as she was more than sure she had, Michelle pushed the button on the intercom. "Mr. Walsh, there is a Ms. Carolina McDonald here to see you; should I send her in?" Michelle asked with all intention to listen to him.

"Yes! Please," Doug responded quickly.

"Hello, Ms. McDonald. How can I help you?" Doug asked.

"That's a matter of reasoning. Hopefully, after I'm finished, you'll still feel the same way because I've worked hard over the years, bringing my two daughters together." Doug was in shock as he had no idea what the woman was implying or assuming, yet he never spoke and continued listening carefully. "And now you have come along and ruined my only chance of putting them together unknowingly. You see Mr. Walsh, when I first met you I was happy because my daughter had found someone of interest.

Doug was dumbfounded. "I'm speaking of Wanda and Rita."

Things were becoming clearer for Doug.

"In case you haven't figured it out. They are half-sisters and they don't know it. So I would appreciate you not revealing it to them. That's the reason you didn't meet my husband when you first came over. He couldn't accept it when I revealed it to him. Therefore, I tell everyone he is out of town on business. I made a mistake and I'm trying to make the most of it by bringing them together. But now you come along and started... excuse my French, screwing them both."

Doug was shocked and wondered how she knew.

"I got someone to get Wanda to let her have a job in the salon. They already feuding and somewhat in comparison to each other's ways and this will completely ruin it. Once they find out you are doing them both. Therefore, I prefer you leave them both alone, so that I can mend them together as I started. I've already lost my husband and I don't want to lose either one of them. I don't expect you to understand, but I do wish you become considerate of the fact since you are disrespecting them in that manner."

Doug was at a loss for words as he didn't know how to respond to her demands or if he should even consider the thought. However, he knew he couldn't afford to let one find out about the other. Yet he needed a very good answer as she looked him deep in the eyes with a hard stare.

"I understand, Ms. McDonald," Doug replied.

"I was hoping you would," she said in a minor tone.

"However, it's not easy undoing what's already done and I don't know how to resolve it other than telling them which only makes matters worse," Doug explained.

"Well, it would be simple to leave them alone," she suggested.

"But, that's easier said than done. How do I go about explaining it to them?" Doug shot back.

"However, I'm sure you'll manage," she said sarcastically.

"I'll see you later and hopefully it's on better terms. And by the way, I see you share the love around here also," she stated nonchalantly.

"I'll do my best, Ms. McDonald," Doug told her.

"I know you will because it wouldn't be in your best interest, otherwise catch my drift?" she said smiling.

Doug was furious amongst other things as he felt lost, threatened and out of sync. Though he had no intention of giving up either of them, he did wonder how he would go about doing it and keeping everyone happy and in the dark? He couldn't believe they were sisters.

CHAPTER 6

Meanwhile, Wanda was preparing a meaningful event of her own for Doug. The event was meant to secure her presence and contain anyone else from invading what she now considered hers. Both women were fighting for his affection and were determined to succeed, unaware that others were also involved. Yet Doug maneuvered and concealed all his antics among them totally undetected or so, he thought.

Nevertheless, he was now concerned about the situation that involved Wanda and Rita. Not to mention the comment Wanda's mother made in his office. He knew he had to do something to ease the tension between them and prevent them from finding out about being related and being intimately involved with him. He was sure it would destroy what he had searched for. But how could he do it? He knew he needed a plan and the only way was to separate them. Something Wanda's mother was not in agreement with and would be furious with. However, that was a chance he was about to take regardless of the consequences or the outcome. It had to be done as soon as possible before it all came back to haunt him later on.

Doug walked into the townhouse shocked at the sight of how things had changed and astonished at the lovely sight of Wanda waiting for him. Dinner was prepared, the lights were low, the music played softly and Wanda was smiling widely as she greeted him with a passionate kiss removing his coat.

Doug lost all his composure for this is how he had always wanted his life to play out. He couldn't believe it was now taking shape and going almost exactly how he planned it. All that was missing was the kids. After dinner and conversation, Doug and Wanda engaged in a night of vigorous pleasing of one another. There was no limit to the others expectation as they totally fascinated each other in every aspect and sexually bonded together. It was a memorable night as Wanda sealed her fate, leaving Doug completely satisfied and confident that the woman of his dreams was right in his face.

They woke the next morning, joyful and happy, thinking about the tactics they employed with each other. Wanda prepared breakfast as Doug prepared for the day. As Doug was in the shower his cell phone rang. Wanda answered it only to discover Rita on the other end. She furiously asked what she's doing with the number. Rita thinking rationally, answers and informs her that she's calling in regards to his cousin's death as an excuse. Wanda then told Rita that Doug was taking a shower, preparing for work and that she would deliver her message before he leaves. Doug exited the shower and dressed, ate breakfast and headed for the office unaware of the phone call.

Upon entering the office, he greeted Michelle with a smile before speaking to one of his clients seated. A few minutes later, Rita entered and addressed Michelle in reference to speaking with a Mr. Doug Walsh. Michelle curiously asked Rita if she had an appointment to which Rita replied no but it was in reference to some real estate she wanted to sell. Then asked if she would be so kind to inform him of her presence. After a few seconds of thought, Michelle asked her to take a seat. She entered the office and returned a minute later, informing her she could be seen now. Rita thanked her and proceeds through the door, feeling the intense stare from the receptionist rendering no thought as to her motive.

"Hello Mr. Walsh!" she said softly.

Doug was in awe at the sight of this lovely young lady's appearance, especially this early in the morning. She was exquisitely dressed in every area unlike he had ever seen her which fascinated him. "Hi Rita, I didn't expect to see you," he said smoothly.

"Did you not receive my message this morning?" she asked curiously.

"What message?" Doug replied.

"I called your cell phone this morning, Wanda answered and said you were in the shower and she would inform you as soon as you came out," Rita said sharply.

Doug knew that wasn't a good sign, how could he had been so careless leaving his cell phone unattended. "I guess she must've forgotten," he shot back.

"Um, I take it she spent the night or has she moved in?" Rita asked seriously, waiting for a reply.

"No, she didn't spend the night and no, she has not moved in either." Doug explained nonchalantly.

"So what was so important?" Doug said quickly changing the subject.

Rita went to the door and locked it. "This!" she replied, opening her coat revealing her nakedness underneath smiling. Doug was in shock as his manhood stood erect at the very instant she exposed her anatomy. Uncontrollably, he rose to his feet and approached the lovely specimen and removed her fur coat. Standing in stilettos she welcomed his every advance.

Doug slowly kissed her lips and caressed her body to the point that his desire took control. He gently laid her across his desk and entered her slowly to the hilt as she wrapped her legs around his waist giving him full access. Doug quickened his pace as she moaned with pleasure to his every stroke, caressing both breast to guide his motion and enhance his fulfillment. While looking into her eyes, Rita was thrilled by the look on his face, giving her the impression he was emotionally overwhelmed and enjoying it as much as her. She moaned louder and louder with each deep thrust until she climaxed with her eyes rolling in the back of her head.

Unaware of the fact that Michelle had turned on his intercom, when she entered the office and heard everything. Doug noticed the intercom clicked off and hurriedly exited Rita, disappointing her from reaching another orgasm.

"What's wrong?" she asked.

"My intercom was on and I'm hoping my receptionist didn't hear us," Doug replied fixing his clothes.

"Don't worry if she enjoyed it half as much as me, she's got to be satisfied," Rita said sheepishly. Doug knew that wouldn't be the case and never responded. After regaining their composure, Doug handed Rita some blank papers and escorted her out the office. As she was leaving, Michelle looked her in the eye to acknowledge her as she left. Doug then grabbed a stack of papers and hit the intercom informing Michelle he needed copies A.S.A.P., in an attempt to discern whether she was listening in or not. Michelle made no notion that she overheard and quickly made the copies. She continued with her normal routine as usual, casually looking sexually into his eyes with a slight grin as she had always done.

However, she now had her homework cut out for her as she

would look into this woman. After Doug left for class, she began her task and discovered more than what interested her. Now, she had leverage as this information would become vital when it was time to use it. There was nothing or no one that could ruin her plans and stop her from obtaining this young stud by any means.

Rita headed into the salon after her romp with Doug sensing negativity from Wanda, and her demeaning stare, due to the expensive fur coat she was wearing. She quickly went to the bathroom and put on her clothes only to come back feeling bad vibes from everyone. She was unaware that Wanda had informed her co-workers of all her little antics that had taken place in the course of a week. She ignored it and proceeded to doing her job, dismissing the thought of what any of them felt or thought about her. She was content with her position in Doug's life, and steadily thought of ways to enhance it even more.

During h lunch break hour, Wanda returned to work from her gynecologist, ecstatic about the news of her being pregnant. She couldn't wait to inform Doug that he was about to become a father. She placed the results into her pocketbook, and thought of motherhood as her mind soared in every direction. She no longer had to fear Rita, or any other women as a threat. She entered the salon exhilarated, and it was obvious to all that change had taken place somewhere, as she flaunted it openly. She kept her belongings in the office, and picked up the phone to call Doug to inform him. Suddenly, she changed her mind when he answered, deciding to tell him directly, to view the expression on his face. Tonight they would celebrate she thought as she hung up, looking frantically as if she was upset.

"Is there something I can help you with?" she asked quickly.

Rita didn't want her thinking she was after her man, so she decided to try to convince her, hoping she would let her guard down long enough for her to make her move. "Wanda, I'm sorry if I caused any discomfort. That was not my intention and I don't want any hard feelings between us over this man. I know he is yours and I am not out to cause you and Doug any problems. It's just that my being involved with his cousin has me feeling somewhat obligated to help find out what happened to him and that's the only reason I called him. Hopefully you understand," she replied in a mild tone.

"I have no problem with that Rita," Wanda exclaimed.

"Good, I just want us to be in agreement," Rita shot back.

Wanda knew she was lying and told her what she wanted to hear. "I understand," Wanda said bluntly.

Rita was sure that was her cue because she was not aware of her motives which would give her a reason to call or even be seen with Doug without any confrontation. This would give her time and full access to work her plan on him as well. Later that night, she knew she had to meet with Redbone so she knew things had to be in order.

While Doug was headed home, his cell phone rang. "Hello!" He answered.

"Mr. Walsh, this is Redbone; I got a tip on what went down with your cousin, but going to have to squeeze some information out of some people to find the culprit," he explained.

"Okay, do whatever. Did you receive your check?" Doug asked frankly.

"Yes!" He shot back.

"Money is no option. Find him and keep me informed when you do," Doug expressed seriously.

"I'll do that, take care," he stated hanging up. Doug was hoping something would come up to find out about what happened to his cousin. But he had no idea of what was really going on and that he was being set up himself. Redbone knew that he had him and all he had to do now was throw the bait. However, he needed everyone in sync and on the same page for his plan to work. So tonight, he would establish all this between them and complete the task. Hopefully, they could pull it off without any problems and sit back and enjoy the fruit of their labor.

Rita looked at her watch, 11:57 P.M. She knew Redbone would be there soon. She then saw headlights beaming towards her as they grew closer. She recognized the car and noticed a second figure in it. Curious as to who it might be, she sat patiently waiting as they eluded her at the moment. "Hi baby! She said as Redbone approached.

"What's up?" he shot back smiling.

"Rita, this is my cousin Michelle. Michelle this is my wife Rita," he said, introducing them, shocked at the sight of the woman before her.

"Hello! I've heard so much about you," Michelle exclaimed. Noticing who she was, she wondered if she recognized her from the office visit with Doug. Evidently not since she was showing no signs of it. Michelle knew she could contain her now because she had something that gave her leverage.

Redbone explained how he had talked to Doug today and told them he doesn't even have a clue as to what happened. Therefore, making their plans much easier to complete. As he was discussing their plan, Rita remembered where she had seen the woman and thought all hell was going to break loose. Michelle noticed the look and figured she must have recognized her and was in shock. After a while of talking, Redbone went to the bathroom as Michelle saw her chance. "I see you recognized who I am now, huh?" she asked roughly.

"Yes, I have," Rita shot back.

"Well, I'm not going to reveal anything so don't worry about that, but for future reference you might not want to be getting intimate with Doug anymore," she told Rita firmly.

"Is that a threat?" Rita asked angrily.

"No, that's a fact. He is off limits to you so don't be fucking him anymore or Redbone might find out," she said.

"Well, let me get something straight, if by chance he does, you might not want to ever see him again because our next meeting won't be pretty. You got that Missy?" Rita said with an intense stare. Michelle laughed as she noticed Redbone heading their way.

"I'm glad ya'll are getting acquainted," he added to the laughter.

"Yes! We have an understanding," Michelle explained.

"That's good, cause we are all going to have to remain focused and on point to get this money," Redbone expressed sharply. Rita was furious and knew she had to complete what she started with Doug because she had other plans that coincided with the one they expressed.

On the other hand, Michelle was happy with the whole arrangement, for she knew she had things under control where as they were totally unaware of at the time.

CHAPTER 7

Wanda was waiting patiently for Doug. She had prepared the ornaments and birthday cake to surprise him. She could not wait to reveal the present she had so anxiously wanted to give him. The minute he walked through the door, she sat smiling as if she was the happiest woman in the world. Doug was indeed surprised that she had gone through all the trouble as he stood there shocked at the sight of the balloons.

"Happy Birthday baby. I'm sure this will be the best one you ever had," Wanda exclaimed smiling.

"And why is that?" Doug asked.

"Because I have a very special present for you," she said. Doug looked down at the wrapped present and thought it couldn't be much from the size of the box.

"Um, is that right?" he said unexcited.

"Yes, and I guarantee it," she said, smiling widely while looking into his eyes. Doug picked up the present and opened it to discover a Rolex. He eagerly thanked Wanda with a long passionate kiss. Wanda told him to blow the candles out and make a wish. Doug was hesitant, but he preceded the honors. They exchanged pieces of cake, feeding one another and laughing. Later, Wanda told him to come receive his real present. She headed towards the bedroom and closed the door. Doug knew that was his cue and headed to the back. As he opened the door, he stood in shock at the sight. Wanda was lying on the bed with only a tee-shirt that read: Baby!

"Are you?" he stuttered.

"Yes, I'm pregnant," she screamed loud. Doug's facial expression went from shock to happiness as he dived to the bed into her arms and kissed her continuously.

"This is what I wanted and you have made me so happy, I love you so much," he expressed excitedly. Wanda couldn't believe how excited and happy he was from hearing the news. She loved every minute of it. Now she knew she need not worry about anything anymore as long as she does her part to make their lives become one. They engaged in passionate lovemaking all night long. Doug woke the next morning thrilled and making plans. He would now become a proud father, something he had always looked forward to and dreamed of all his life.

It was now unfolding before him and becoming a reality. There was so much in front of him that had to be done and no matter how busy he was, it took second priority to this new development. They both were overwhelmed and looked forward to the arrival, opting not to tell everyone just yet. Doug knew that's what was on Wanda's mind from the look on her face. He had to convince her not to reveal this to anyone yet because he didn't want to create any problems just yet. He knew once her mother finds out he would have more than enough to deal with anyway.

"Wanda, I don't think we should tell anyone because we don't need any distractions right away," Doug expressed.

"Why not baby?" she asked concerned.

"Just let them find out when the time comes," he said bluntly.

"But what about my mom?" she asked seriously.

"Let it be a surprise to her too, that way by the time you are showing, I'll have everything in order," Doug said.

"What you mean in order?" she shot back.

"That's my surprise, just trust me," Doug asked politely.

"Okay, I trust you," Wanda expressed, while thinking of what he really meant.

Doug was elated that she was in agreement being that he needed all the time he could muster to start preparing for what was about to surface. He somehow had to manage keeping her mother out of the equation as much as possible and he knew that wouldn't be an easy task under the circumstances. After their conversation, he prepared for the day ahead, kissed Wanda and joyfully headed through the door; smiling as if he had won the lottery. Things were taking shape and getting better, he thought. As time went by, things remained normal and Doug escaped the turmoil of destroying Wanda and Rita ever coming together, even as their mother was furious.

After months of explaining to everyone and keeping things intact, they eventually got around any confusion that arose. Although her mother was upset, the damage had been done and there was nothing she could do but accept it. Rita was devastated when she figured out Wanda was expecting Dougs' child, but that didn't change the way she felt or decrease her interest for Doug. She knew as long as he wasn't married, he was open game. That was her intention from the beginning; to try and put matching rings on their fingers by any means necessary regardless of whether Wanda had his child or not.

Douglas Antonio Walsh was born August 18, 1992, weighing 6 lbs 12oz and in perfect health. The baby was an enhancement to them both in every aspect. They cherished him and increased their desire for one another through mutual respect of creating a life together. Doug moved Wanda into his house and they shared the responsibility of raising their son together. He later rented the townhouse for Rita, securing her presence. Unaware that he actually put Rita in the townhouse, Wanda was happy with his decision for her and the baby to move into the estate.

Meanwhile, Rita was watching as things were also unfolding in her favor as well. It made it easier for her to work her plan as she would betray her husband and his cousin in the end. She was, however, unaware that she was also being betrayed. They were all wearing masks and not revealing their true selves by any means under the circumstances. But in the end who would win? Being that no one knew of the others plans. Nevertheless, they continued pursuing their task together while separately and indirectly manipulating one another for selfish gain. Redbone had no intention of his plan being split three ways. Michelle had no intention of sharing any money since she was in full control. However, Rita had a card none of them had, she had his heart.

With that alone, she felt she could reach deeper and more effectively. Therefore, her hands were full as much as Doug frequently visited her in the townhouse. She knew she had to step up another notch or she could never contend with Wanda and there was only one sure fire way... get pregnant.

The very next day, Rita phoned the travel agency and made reservations to Cancun Mexico. Her plan was to tell Doug she won the trip and convince him to accompany her; all expenses paid. Then she would accomplish her mission in three days and four nights. However, her work was cut out for her and she knew her time was already limited with Doug. That night she put on a red negligee and patiently waited with strawberries and whip cream, watching a movie and contemplating how she would perform. When suddenly the door knob turned slowly as Doug entered the corridor, his eyes grew large as her smile widened in excitement. Their eyes locked together as they both aroused each other's desires. Rita motioned with her hand for Doug to come over, with her other hand she held her lips informing him not to speak.

As he sat beside her on the sofa, she dipped one strawberry into the whip cream and pushed it halfway in his mouth. After he bit half, she then licked the remaining cream from his lips and pushed her tongue deep down his throat while rubbing her hand directly on his manhood. Arousing his desire to new heights, she unzipped his pants and removed his swollen rod, lowering herself and gradually taking him by surprise. She put her lips around his enlarged head sucking ever so gently, forcing him to tense, physically bracing himself. She picked up the pace as she rubbed whip cream over his penis, enjoying it as much as he was.

Filled with desire, she came to her knees and straddled her legs across him and inserted the head between her lips and glided down slowly until reaching the base of his pelvis moaning. She stroked slowly up and down while looking into his eyes. Doug then pulled the gown over her head, caressing her breast firmly. Arousing Rita to stroke harder and guiding her, she reached an orgasm thunderously moaning loud, collapsing into his arms, and jerking frantically. Slowly she laid on his side. Doug exited her gently sliding down and parting the lips of her pussy slowly licking around them teasing her before he reached her clit, twirling his tongue around it in slow motion, sucking gently before pushing his tongue to her clit and twirling inside her finding her G-spot. Rita was totally vulnerable and out of control. She raised both legs giving him total access.

As Doug put his tongue deeper, she moaned louder and louder reaching her peak. Sensing this, Doug withdrew his tongue, stopping before she reached it. He then pulled the head of his dick up and down her clit as she jumped at the touch. Slowly pushing in, he reached down and held both legs up high while furiously pounding hard strokes deep into her, making slapping sounds with every thrust. Rita moaned louder and with every stroke held on tighter to his arms. Doug continued pounding and slowed down before ejaculation, only to pound harder. As he could tell, she enjoyed his tactic as much as he did. Amazed at the excitement he had for her, Rita eagerly took everything he had to offer her gracefully thrusting herself up to meet his strokes, until they both reached an enormous orgasm together and collapsed in each others arms.

They lay motionless for minutes while sliding into a relaxing state, feeling one another emotionally. They connected to new heights sexually while physically creating a true bond that would become routine. After lying in each other's arms, still connected sexually, Rita looked into his eyes and revealed that she won a trip. Carefully watching his reaction, she asked him to accompany her to Cancun, Mexico. After a moment of reflecting, Doug answered yes, while thinking that he needed time to think and relax a little.

Rita was thrilled that her plan was working. She kissed him lightly and put her hands upon his as if motioning him to finish the job. Doug obliged and slowly glided in and out while looking in her eyes as she made grateful facial expressions which enhanced the pleasure of their lovemaking that much more. During the night, he thought about how he would manage spending that much time away without anyone becoming curious as to what was going on. However, he knew he could find a solution, but he didn't want Wanda suspicious of his whereabouts. Then all of a sudden it hit him, he knew just what to do when morning came and he got to work. He fell asleep pleased after performing his normal routine.

When he got to his office, Doug faxed a realtor in Cancun concerning the purchase of some land and property. Leaving his home fax number for a return call, knowing they would be interested and return the fax for Wanda to see. Therefore, giving him an airtight alibi to spend time in Mexico with Rita. He continued getting things in order while he reflected on last night until Michelle broke his concentration as she walked in and suggested lunch.

"Where did you have in mind?" he asked.

"I feel like seafood," she said softly.

"Red Lobster's calling me."

They retreated to Red Lobster and ordered. While waiting, Doug noticed Cassandra walk through the door being escorted by whom he thought must have been her husband. They were seated three tables away, facing him. He suddenly lost his appetite as he was overwhelmed by her striking beauty. He never thought he would see her again, but then she made eye contact which was sufficient enough for him, for he knew he had at least been recognized. Hopefully, they would meet again on better terms.

After lunch, Doug and Michelle returned to the office and entered only to find the place rather crowded. Business as usual, they proceeded in accompanying their patrons before Doug left for class. Doug was close to graduation and eager to finish so he could move on with his desperately needed spare time. Once he arrived to class, he took pride in completing whatever was set before him. But he wasn't ready for the confrontation he was about to receive. As he was seated, he noticed a young woman smiling in his direction. He was unaware that she was even in the class before now. She was very appealing to say the least, as she approached.

"Hello, I'm new here and I couldn't help noticing you are somewhat humble in your ways," she stated sharply.

"Now, how did you arrive at that conclusion?" Doug shot back as he found her unconvincing.

"Because I have watched you closely for the past week and I am a good judge of character," she exclaimed.

Curiously Doug asked, "What's your name?"

"I'm sorry, it's Veronica Howge," she stated, making his acquaintance.

Doug was charmed by the young lady's demeanor, but felt she was a bit forward with her approach. He felt he had to find the central point and motivating force of why she decided to make herself known to him. "May I ask why you have been observing me?" he stated looking directly into her big brown eyes.

"Because I sensed an acute connection that was pleasant so I decided to find out if my assumption was right. Although it may seem forward, I have no problem seeking what interest me," she said calmly. "Besides, I'm new in town and I don't know anyone,"

Doug was upset, but showed no signs, choosing to see where she was going instead, being that she had potential. "That's understandable and I'm glad to make your acquaintance as well. My name is Doug Walsh," he said.

"I know! I already did my homework in that department. But I'm anxious to see what else you have in store because I'm free after class; and don't have a way home today. In other words, I would appreciate it if you would be so kind to give me one," she asked politely.

"Do you always come on to people so easily?" Doug asked.

"Under the circumstances, no, but I am comfortable with you and feel good about it," she said nonchalantly. Doug decided to get to know this exquisite looking young lady and offered to give her a ride home after class.

He was eager to see how far he could actually go or what she would permit him to do once they arrived. He escorted her to his car and drove to her apartment some ten blocks from campus. She invited him in and offered him a drink while she went into her bedroom. Returning casually dressed in some skin tight shorts, exposing her ass cheeks and a small tee shirt barely covered her firm breast. Doug became excited as soon as she entered the room, trying to hold his composure. However, her intentions were obvious as she bent over, exposing her ass while reaching for the remote to turn on the stereo system, giving him full access to her anatomy. She sat close and started talking about herself in a way that expressed her loneliness.

Doug read her every intention and fed on her vulnerability as she poured drink after drink knowing she was tipsy. He moved closer and put his arms around her as she fell slowly into his chest rubbing his rib cage. She made her way to his lips and kissed him passionately giving him the invitation he had been waiting for since the moment she exposed her pretty brown ass in front of him.

They made their way to her bedroom and engaged in some energetic sex that had Doug totally off balanced. He never would have thought she was the type to engage in such a manner. She performed kinky things that he had never experienced with any other woman. Nevertheless, he was actually enjoying her performance in ways he never felt before and totally unaware that she was videotaping the entire scenario secretly. Exhausted, they lay there looking at the mirrors and over the room while conversing about their lives, when suddenly a loud click erupted and startled Doug.

"What was that noise?" he asked curiously.

"It was probably the heating system," she told him. Doug thought no more of the incident and decided to head for the office. He showered with her and dressed while making plans to see her again before they parted. Excited about his new prospect he still felt that something was rather peculiar the way things had suddenly taken place so quickly, but he dismissed the thought and went with the flow.

CHAPTER 8

Doug and Rita spent three glorious nights and four fun fulfilled days in Cancun, Mexico exploring one another's most intimate desires. They barely left the bedroom other than occasionally dining out and seeking the exotic sights of the area. They experienced how much they had in common and made an everlasting impact upon each other in ways they never knew existed between them. Uninterrupted, they enjoyed every minute of being alone until Rita revealed what was going on and how she never intended for things to get out of hand.

Doug was now furious because he never once suspected Michelle to be so devious. He had no idea Redbone was behind the death of his cousin and now he wondered how he could actually trust the woman he had come to care so much about in such a little time. Mentally, he was at the crossroads and wasn't quite sure how he would handle the situation. Wondering whether he should reveal to Rita what he knew about her and Wanda also crossed his mind. He chose not to open up while he desperately thought about his next move to straighten out where he had been wronged.

He couldn't believe the ones he trusted were betraying him and he had no intentions of letting it continue to happen. But how was he going to go about doing things in the proper manner and remain clear of danger or trouble now that others knew about what was happening? Regardless of the consequences, they had gone way too far and someone was going to pay dearly for it. He acquired all the information from Rita that he could obtain and she revealed everything including her marriage to Redbone. Now that he felt more comfortable about the whole ordeal, he wanted to reveal to her that Wanda was her half-sister. If he did this, he believed they would be more willing to help him complete his task of getting even before they complete their plans against him. But he decided against it until he had them together.

Michelle had access to all his assets and business deals, and knew his whole operation, which made it easy for her to do major damage. Also, her cousin Redbone, who had mega street ties in every area could destroy him physically. Now he had to get a step ahead and fast, but he didn't want them in any way curious as to his knowing about their plot. Therefore, he had Rita continue as usual and keep him abreast as to what was going on at all times. Totally convinced she had won her way into his heart, she was more than willing and eager to stand by his side to the end.

As they returned, things turned again as Wanda had discovered brochures from Cancun, Mexico at Rita's work station in the salon and became suspicious. She was furious at the possibility that Rita went along with Doug on his trip (which only made matters worse). Doug noticed a difference in her actions, but didn't bother commenting on the way she was acting towards him because he had other things to worry about. He went about his daily routines as usual. However, he sensed something wasn't right and never entertained the thought of her knowing anything.

Meanwhile, Wanda was making moves of her own to secure what she felt was stripped away from her. She knew she must take drastic measures to control her interest and secure her son's future.

She decided to apply pressure on Doug to marry her so that they could become one complete family together. Everyone had a motive, yet only Doug knew the full extent of what was actually going on now or at least that's what he was lead to believe. However, there were other events on the horizon, he had not yet foreseen or even imagined. After months and months of these events transpiring before him, he managed to keep things under control and in the proper prospective as he continued to counter their plans. How long they would pursue this before cashing in was anybody's guess being that it would have to be done correctly without leaving a paper trail, which was no easy task.

Michelle acted normal, as if everything was the same. Redbone kept constant contact as if he was really working to find who killed Jerry. Rita kept Doug informed of their every move just as she promised, constantly remaining sincere to Doug. Doug had made some major adjustments of his own through contacts he had obtained over the years. He was almost set for them to come and create havoc before they knew what had hit them.

However, he wanted to remain discreet in the way things were handled and avoid any contact that would get his hands dirty. The process would take a while and he perfected it well. So, he patiently watched and waited until they made a fatal mistake. Surprisingly, greed got the best of them as Michelle had her contacts accumulating even more property for Doug to purchase. Aware of her intent, he went along with whatever she presented and noticed how skillful she actually was as she conducted business.

Doug noticed an enormous increase in his assets and was in some way pleased at her results, but furious that she was the main one out to rob him blind. He knew that they would eventually pay for it in the end.

In the years to come, things really got hectic. His life with Wanda and his son took the majority of his time as he constantly dealt with her concerns of getting married. At the same time, he also concealed his relationship with Rita along with the fact that she and Wanda were half-sisters. In addition, he was keeping her in check as he prevented her husband and his cousin Michelle from robbing him blind. Along with the new interest, Veronica kept him on edge at all times and was becoming more demanding daily.

Time was really hard for him to find and couldn't, in no way, be wasted now for any reason. They kept getting better as Doug became the host of a hip-hop video show, giving him access to promote clubs. He sometimes held shows and dance competitions at local clubs around town; increasing their attendance and providing a huge amount of exposure.

This, however, made a tremendous impact for Doug. He had become somewhat of a local celebrity and gained a lot of attention. Only now he had more women flocking to be around him and he took advantage of it whenever possible, creating even more havoc. His night club was where everybody wanted to be and now it stayed crowded every night. He befriended a radio host, Mike Dawson, a local DJ who he used to help him establish a wide fan base. Mike was married with two kids and well known since he started out in radio and played clubs in his spare time. Things blossomed for Doug and he prospered in every aspect of his life. He finally began to feel content as his life took shape.

He was sitting in his den one night and not expecting anyone when his doorbell rang. He was shocked at the sight of Redbone, being that he couldn't understand how greed could move a man to do things that wasn't logical. He had been constantly milking him for money while pretending to be on the trail of his cousin's killer and now it was getting irritating. Doug had already paid him well over $200,000.00 and he kept coming for more as if he had really been working to find the culprit. He was virtually unaware that Doug knew he was the culprit that killed his cousin. It had to end. How much longer would he continue, Doug thought.

"Do you have some information for me?" Doug asked, knowing what he wanted.

"Yes! And I'm sorry to drop in at such hour, but I felt this needed to be handled A.S.A.P. I got a tip that your cousin was dealing with some Dominicans out of New York and I'm headed that way. Therefore, I need you to accommodate for the trip," he told him.

Doug almost went ballistic at the thought of him invading his home and presenting such a lame con game to swindle him out of more money. Instead, he remained calm and went along with it.

"How much do you need?" Doug asked concerned.

"Well, I'm taking a couple of guys along; therefore we may be there for a week. So it might take around fifty grand," he stated flatly.

Anger rose to new heights within Doug as his heart pounded heavily. He knew that this was his way of manipulating him out of cash. Doug curtailed his resentment and decided to give him another fifty grand.

"Alright! Have a seat, I'll be a minute," he said slowly. Doug went upstairs to his bedroom and opened his safe, returning with a fifty thousand stack of hundred dollar bills. He returned downstairs where Redbone sat on the sofa, unaware that Wanda had been sitting in the other room listening to the whole conversation. Doug handed the money over to Redbone as he sat directly in front of him. He then pushed his hand down into the cushion of the sofa placing his hand upon a 9mm Beretta.

"There comes a time when it's better to start from the end to the beginning," Doug told him.

Totally in awe at the comment, Redbone didn't have a clue as to what Doug meant. "Excuse me?" he asked, trying to discern what Doug meant.

"A man's got to know his limitations," Doug continued.

"I agree and I guarantee the bastard will pay for what he did,"

Redbone shot back cleverly.

"I know he will because his time has just run out," Doug stated with a cold stare.

Suddenly, Redbone sensed something wrong and reached for his gun. Doug was already a step ahead and placed the 9mm at the front of his head pulling the trigger. Blood and brains splattered everywhere. Suddenly he heard Wanda scream loudly, unaware that she had viewed the entire scenario. She came into the room shocked upon realizing that Doug had murdered the man in their house. He then calmed her down and explained why he had done it; revealing details he hoped she understood since they involved Rita. Someone she wasn't too fond of in the first place. However, he couldn't bring himself to reveal the most shocking secret, as he wasn't sure how or if she would accept it.

After minutes of explaining and calming Wanda, Doug knew he had to dispose of the body and clean up the mess it created. But first, he had Wanda assure him that she would never tell anyone because if she did this would ruin them spending their lives together as a complete family.

"What do you mean by a complete family?" she asked, wanting to clarify his statement.

"Happily married with children," he stated sharply. The words she had wanted to hear had been spoken and she had no problem sealing the promise. Doug knew that was the only way to assure him she would never reveal the murder to anyone since that's what she always wanted. However, he hadn't decided as to when he would actually marry her and at the rate things were going, he knew it wouldn't be anytime soon. He had the body exposed and covered with cement on the estate without anyone's knowledge. Now he would monitor the actions of Michelle and Rita as they contemplate the disappearance of Redbone. He thought only Rita would become suspicious, but she would not accuse him anyway, since she wasn't in agreement to comply with him and his lifestyle to say the least.

After weeks went by, Doug sensed Michelle's weariness as she expressed concern regarding not hearing from Redbone. He informed her he hadn't heard from him since he last told him about a trip to New York. Putting her on a chase to nowhere and dismissing her from thinking otherwise concerning his whereabouts. He had already heard Rita complaining somewhat about him a few nights after the incident took place. But that didn't really sound as though she was worried or actually cared.

Nevertheless, he knew he wouldn't have to worry about his body turning up anywhere and eventually they both would think he took the money and ran out on them. That suited Doug just fine as he had the major part of his plan completed. Now all that was left to do was to obtain rightful ownership of his real estate and retrieve the assets that Michelle had unlawfully obtained from him. Killing her wasn't an option in order to retain what was rightfully his, therefore, he had to do things in a clever fashion where she would never detect what he was up to, trying to acquire the information needed. He knew there was no time to waste.

Doug started acquiring his records, and made contacts with people associated in his real estate holdings throughout the banks he did his business with, hiding it from Michelle in the process. He had his auntie Ruth do some checking of her own since she knew the majority of his holdings. She made some interesting discoveries that were indeed hidden very well. However, she found ways of getting information through contacts she had made over the years selling real estate. Although the process was time consuming and somewhat confidential in certain aspects, it took months on end to track the vital information she sought. She introduced Doug to the people who could likely help him in the areas he needed to obtain legal ownership from Michelle.

Michelle had done a magnificent job in handling and hiding the finances of his assets somewhat legally. However, it was very complex and took an enormous amount of time and thought sorting through every angle precisely to redo what she had perfectly arranged. He wanted to do this before she caught wind of his moves and correct it.

CHAPTER 9

Doug continued pursuing his interest over the year and his family prospered happily together. He still kept his relationship with Rita, Veronica and a host of others, he had acquired through his nightclub and stints as the host of his hip-hop video show. The nightclub had flourished tremendously and provided him with a cushion financially. All the while, he kept Michelle in check, unaware of what had taken place and what he was attempting beyond her knowledge.

Wanda seemed happy and content. She was well aware of his flings as she started discovering small things that had signs of other women written all over them. And even though she was hesitant to address it, she still kept record of it all. However, there was only so much she could take. Therefore, she started leaving notes, making it known that she was aware of his escapades. She started following Doug and sneaking around on her own, watching his actions when time permitted, without his knowledge. However, she wasn't making accusations; she had firsthand knowledge and pure facts. This didn't sit well with Doug as he couldn't figure out how she was acquiring this information as it was disrupting his flow. And that was something he didn't need right now. He tried occupying her time by keeping her close so that he could know where she was at all times. But that only gave her more reason to complain about how other women acted around him. He then realized how insecure she really was and decided to spend more quality time with her on the Island of St. Thomas.

They spent every second together never parting. He assured her that she was his future wife and that no other woman could claim that part of his heart because it belonged to her. She fell head over heels and enjoyed every bit of it to the point that she changed her total outlook. This really pleased Doug as he felt he had escaped most of the drama by securing her love for him. Now he had to uphold his end, but he still had no intentions of changing what he was doing just yet. However, he knew he had to tone it down where it wasn't visible to keep things in order.

Things went well until one night Wanda went to her mother's house to pick up her son. On the way home, she had to make a detour due to an accident on the freeway. She exited the ramp, familiar with the area, she drove right down the street she had lived on. She then noticed Doug exiting his car at the townhouse where she used to stay. She hit the brakes and pulled over, watching as he let himself in with the key just as he had done when she lived there.

Curious as to what he was doing there, she decided to wait. After close to an hour, she saw no sign of Doug exiting the house. She then dialed his cell phone, as he answered, she inquired about his whereabouts and how long before he gets home. Doug informed her he was on his way out of the office, heading there at that moment. Wanda accepted the lie and hung up. She was furious as she now knew he had some other woman staying where she had been staying and that he was being disloyal and lying to her immensely. This really set her off.

Wanda hurried home only to find a stranger in the driveway parked. She carefully watched him before she decided to exit the car with her son. As she opened her door and retrieved her son from his car seat, the man approached.

"Hello, I didn't mean to startle you. I'm a friend of Jerry's, Doug's cousin and I really need to see Doug ASAP. I've been here over an hour. He isn't answering his cell phone and I have a flight out of here in an hour. Things are not going well and I don't have time to explain or even involve you for that matter. Can you give Doug this suitcase and tell him that it's too hot for me and that I have to bounce right now?" the man said with a torrid look on his face.

Wanda was now afraid as the man looked as if someone was seriously after him. She accepted the suitcase as the man raced off like a ghost. After securing her son in the house, she went to retrieve the suitcase. Still fuming from catching Doug, her curiosity took over as she opened the suitcase. Her discovery almost made her faint as she noticed a large bag of cocaine and under it sat the most money she had ever seen in her life. She quickly hid the suitcase as she had no intentions of giving it to Doug, at least not right now anyway. Doug came in about ten minutes behind her and acted as if nothing was wrong. Something she knew he was absolutely good at. So she remained normal as if things were alright. They ate dinner, put their son to bed and made love as if they hadn't seen one another for a long time. She knew that was to justify what he had done and even though she was mad at him, she wasn't about to argue with that kind of attention. She really enjoyed and appreciated his desire.

The next morning after dropping her son off and heading to the salon to check on things, she decided to go by the townhouse and knock on the door. As it opened, she noticed a young woman with long black hair and an hourglass figure. Instantly, she asked the woman about an assumed person staying there. The young woman let her know that she did not know this particular individual. Therefore, Wanda excused herself and headed to work.

Doug had only recently moved Veronica into the townhouse opting to let Rita stay in one of his houses in Raleigh. Little did Wanda know that if she had come three days earlier, she would have seen Rita answer that same door and her reception would have been totally different. Now she planned to find ways to affect the way Doug operated and there was no limit to her deviousness. She hired a private investigator to keep tabs on his every move. She also paid someone to set fire to the nightclub to curb his nights away from home.

Knowing he would never suspect her of doing anything of that nature, she constantly made excuses about everything to devote his actions to her and their son. She created havoc everywhere she turned, demanding that he give his family his undivided attention and making an impact with her own sexual escapades to convince him otherwise. Although it was working, it also prevented Doug from keeping things intact as he once did. This cramped his style in more ways than he could handle under the circumstances.

In time, eventually things became worse as he became depressed and agitated at her charades. Things constantly went sour as Wanda started confronting Doug about the other women he was involved with and creating havoc whenever confrontation arose, constantly making his life a living hell.

However, this only made matters worse as he continued doing whatever he desired since there were opportunities everywhere he turned. Wanda became outraged at his escapades and found relief in the suitcase that was left for Doug by Jerry's friend Leroy. She opened the bag of cocaine and started snorting its contents. Amazed at the results, she kept engaging to the point that she became overwhelmed at how it made her feel total relief.

Eventually she got caught up as this became a part of her daily routine and she started neglecting her work or care anymore for that matter. She relieved herself of any thoughts about what was going on until she became delirious. Doug noticed that her complaints had stopped, but he never saw the odd behavior as she hid that very well while he was around. However, he began to notice that she wasn't spending much time with their son, opting to let her mother watch him for periods of time which he thought was unusual. She began losing weight and neglecting to keep herself up as time went by claiming she was sick. Doug became suspicious and one day he came home early and discovered a powdery substance on the mirror on the coffee table. He then confronted her as he knew from the taste that it was cocaine.

"Wanda! He screamed loudly." As she slowly came down the stairs high from the effects of the drug looking distraught, he asked, "Are you doing cocaine?"

"What the hell do you care? I sit around here and you act as though I don't exist; constantly running around with other woman, neglecting the family that truly loves you," she started crying.

"Baby, that's not true. I do love my family, that means the world to me," he shouted.

"Well, you have a hell of a way of showing it. I know about your affairs. I've had a private investigator following you everywhere," she threw a stack of pictures at him. "Now, how can you stand there and tell me you love me Doug when you don't spend time with me? You don't make love to me and you show me no attention," she expressed heatedly.

Staring at the pictures, Doug's shock soon gave way to anger. "That's still no excuse for you destroying your life. You have responsibilities and obligations that require you to remain stable and a son that needs to be properly loved and cares for. There is nothing you could possibly want for around here, anyone would cherish what you have right now," he barked angrily.

Wanda walked up to his face, looked him directly in his eyes and stared for a long moment before she spoke her mind.

"Doug, anyone can view a subject literary and arrive at that conclusion based on the materialistic things they actually see. But at this point I would challenge their misconceptions. Because none of this truly can make you happy without someone that loves you and be present when you need them. But you don't understand that because you are so caught up in yourself thinking the world revolves around you and that's not the case. I have needs and feelings too. So if you expect me to stay here and accept what you are doing, it's not going to happen," she stated seriously.

"What do you mean Wanda?" Doug asked concerned.

"I mean I'm leaving and you can continue to run around freely, that way I don't have to put up with it anymore. I can make a life of my own with no disturbance of that kind. I've been loyal to you and this is how you show your gratitude. Well, that's not acceptable to me," she shot back.

This was not an option for Doug. He did not want to lose her and his son amongst various other things he was concerned about involving her. He had to think quickly. "Alright, I understand you are upset and I was wrong. I apologize, please forgive me. I don't want you to go anywhere. We can work things out. Cocaine isn't the way. It will destroy you and you have too much to lose," he exclaimed softly.

"I don't have a damn thing to lose because it's already gone and you are not going to change because it's not in you to subject yourself to someone else's demands so stop playing games. I don't need you in my life. I want to be happy and I'm not, therefore, I'm moving on and in time I hope you find whatever it is that you are looking for cause it's obviously not me," Wanda expressed crying.

Doug was furious that she had her mind completely made up and nothing he said worked; and the thought of her taking his son with her devastated him even more. "I'm hoping you reconsider and give me another chance to show you that I am sincere," Doug said honestly. However, she knew that was a front and if she gave him another chance right now it would only end in the same results. Although she really didn't want to leave, she knew she must for a little while and make him come to grips with reality.

"My mind is made up as I have thought long and hard while sitting alone here many nights and I am going to go take some time to find myself because I am feeling rather lost. Our son will be with my mother and you can do whatever you want. As for the incident with Redbone, I'll take that to my grave, you never have to worry. I love you deeply, that's why I must go. I hope you respect and understand that because it's the truth," she said staring in his eyes.

Doug was standing there completely numb because he was about to lose the woman of his dreams. Knowing she wasn't about to listen to anything he said at the moment, he collected his thoughts carefully. "I can accept that, but I don't want you to go, please reconsider and take it into consideration for the sake of our son. This isn't all about us, he deserves to have a mother and father figure in his life," Doug reasoned.

"Well, you picked a fine time to make that assumption and as much as I know you are right, I can't bring myself to believe that's really in your heart. Therefore, I feel we need some time apart to collect our thoughts and then figure out exactly what we want together because as of right now you have no sense of direction that's in the best interest of us being a complete family. And I can't accept being put through any more humiliation."

"Where will you go?" he asked.

"I haven't decided. I just need time to ponder my thoughts and provide for myself and my son," she moaned somberly.

"But that's already established. Our son will never want for anything," he shot back.

"Except the love of his caring parents, which he doesn't have right now. Nevertheless, I meant emotionally, cause I'm a wreck that's not fully functional to care for him in the proper manner due to the stress and anger that's built up with me dealing with you in this relationship. It's obvious you have no knowledge of how in depth I truly love you, and I understand that we just might not live up to one another's expectations. But I have always expected to become your wife as you promised. That has taken second fiddle and eluded you for the last four years or so," she said angrily.

"So this is what it's all about?" Doug asked sharply.

"Partially and various other things I won't comment on being that you already know what they are," she shouted back.

"This is nothing we can't fix," Doug told her as he grasped her shoulders, pleading for another chance.

"I agree, but not right now. I need time alone and I can't neglect myself any longer," she reasoned.

Thoughts went through his mind racing as he held her and looked deep into her eyes. Could it be someone else? He erased the thought, knowing it wasn't worth questioning her about."Who will run the salon while you are away?" he asked.

"I'll find someone trustworthy," she exclaimed calmly.

"Let Rita handle it," Doug suggested.

Suddenly rage entered her like a bolt of lightning. The fact that he could even mention her while they were in an emotional state as severe as this at this moment. "Like she's been handling you," she said angrily.

"What's that's supposed to mean?" he shot back, not realizing he had opened a can of worms for himself.

"I saw her in this house sucking your dick and neither of you knew I was even here, so don't question my integrity by playing me to the left anymore," she told him.

Doug had absolutely no idea she had any knowledge of him being involved with Rita and that created even more problems. How could he now inform her about them being half-sisters? The shit had hit the fan and he knew only time would mend what he had let get out of hand. He saw no reason denying anything anymore, she knew it all.

"Once again, I'm sorry and apologize for any harm or discomfort that I have caused you. Hopefully in time, you will find it in your heart to forgive me and return home and let me make up for what I've done wrong," he expressed sincerely. As he hugged her tightly she looked in his eyes and walked up the stairs to retrieve the suitcases she had already packed. She told him she would keep in touch before she left out the door. As she pulled off, she began crying for she never wanted to leave, yet she had a sudden feeling of satisfaction that felt as though a ton had been lifted off her shoulders.

Doug now turned the tables and had a private investigator follow her to keep tabs on her whereabouts. Both were distraught with fear of losing the other and totally unaware of how much they each regretted what happened. They had a tremendous amount of stress build up that had to be dealt with in some shape, form or fashion. Wanda went to a far off island resort and gazed at the sun, literally drowning in misery and hiding from the truth as a way of coping with the disaster. She was still ruining herself with cocaine and gaining an expensive habit. As she binged for weeks on end, Doug had photographs of her in some exotic places with people around her constantly.

He knew she eventually would come home when her money ran low. However, he had no idea that wasn't about to happen anytime soon. Nevertheless, the way he was dealing with her loss was taking an effect on him in ways he couldn't handle as well. Indulging himself more in his relationships only made matters worse as he couldn't replace the part of his heart he had lost. There was absolutely no substitute for Wanda and he knew he had to have her back. He eventually made an appointment to see a therapist and started weekly visits that helped ease the pain.

Then tragedy struck and he received a phone call informing him that Wanda had been admitted to the hospital where it was discovered that the cocaine had slowed the pace of her heart making it almost impossible to function on her own. However, she eventually recovered and he placed her in an expensive rehab program, visiting and checking on her progress as she gained her strength. He wanted her in tip top shape before she would be released from the rehab facility.

Doug had taken on every challenge as life became hectic and tumultuous. And he kept a close eye on Wanda's progress, along with seeing his therapist regularly, coping with everything that had taken place. He began feeling a bit of relief. Then suddenly, his therapist asked that he see someone she knew that was more experienced to help him with his problems. Doug, however, was not amused or comfortable with the idea. He knew he would have to explain all of his problems over again to another total stranger. After some thinking, he agreed with her decision and decided to see the new doctor next week.

He entered the office dressed to impress as he knew he only had one chance to make his first impression. Once there, the receptionist; a young lady fresh out of college asked his name and informed him to have a seat. As he sat, he noticed the office had walls full of black urban art. Admiring it, he thought the woman had good taste in that area when suddenly the receptionist told him that he could go in now. Upon entering her office, Doug became amazed at the size of her office. He noticed a woman sitting in a big office chair with her back to him typing on the computer.

As she heard him enter, she continued working on the computer. Introducing herself, but never turning around. "Hello Mr. Walsh, I'm Dr. Amy Williams. I hope that I can be of service to you as I already have your records and recorded conversations with your last therapist. Have a seat, I'll only be a minute," she told him. Doug sat as he continued admiring her office and the picture of a lovely little girl that sat upon her desk. This gave him indications that she must be happily married or at least involved with someone. As she finished she turned her computer off and slowly swiveled around to face him. Doug eyes became the size of quarters as he thought he was now in Heaven. The sight of this beautiful lady had him mesmerized to the point he was happy just being there.

"Sorry, I didn't mean to keep you waiting. I had to personally put you in the computer. As I inform all of my clients that our sessions are strictly confidential. I am glad to finally meet you as I noticed you have a complex problem that I once had to deal with myself. This is why you were referred to me and I am sure I can help you overcome it," she concluded.

Dazed at the sight of her he was at a loss for words. She was a magnificent specimen, young and beautiful. He couldn't wait to see her stand and reveal the rest of her body. "Thanks, I really need help dealing with it now," he said in a way he hoped was convincing. All the while entertaining the other thoughts currently running through his mind.

After an hour of discussion, the session ended and they both agreed that it went well. She stood and walked around her desk, revealing her sleek brown skinned body. She was tremendous and had a swagger that showed she was very confident with it. Doug was amazed and overwhelmed at how lovely she actually was before him. He couldn't resist thinking about her sexually. She was no more than five or six years older. He shook her hand as he informed her he looked forward to the next visit. Upon leaving, he couldn't wait to do his homework on her and find out all he possibly could to get closer to her.

Doug had an appointment the next day with the manager at Bank of America in reference to his business dealings. A tip he received from his auntie Ruth through her connections. However, Doug already knew her. He was to meet a Ms. Yvonne Spivey, a 26 year old bank manager who had credentials in various areas of banking; a very attractive, intelligent woman on the rise in the corporate world and confident in her potential. She was happily married now and had a son. She was ambitious in every way, fresh into her marriage and making strides to reach perfection. She and Doug had become quick platonic friends as she gave him legal advice concerning his finances.

After 2 years of friendship, her spirit dwindled and she left her husband after he confessed to cheating on her and catching gonorrhea from another woman. He had constantly tried to control her using her son as a crutch and tearing down her self-esteem as she prospered; becoming independent and moving up enormously fast at a young age. However, this was to her advantage as she finally had reason to leave him now. Suddenly, she blossomed as her life soared to new heights. She focused on her career, as it became demanding, along with her son, that she stayed single for many years.

After enduring all the ill treatment for the sake of her son, separating at that time wasn't an option as she tried keeping hope alive. She became depressed one day when she had to turn down one of her friends from college on a loan for her struggling nightclub. Then she refused to give up finding a solution. Her friend Zerita Goddfrey was very special to her and she wasn't about to let her down if she could help.

Mimi as she called her convinced Yvonne to invest her money and become part owner with her. The idea was far fetched in her line of work, Yvonne thought. But after careful consideration, she reviewed her options and came up with a plan. She started spending time whenever possible discussing the idea with Doug, who gave her vital information concerning the management of a club and came up with a way they could promote it and increase their clientele tremendously. She decided to give it a try and let Doug set things in motion since he had already experienced the ins and outs of running a successful nightclub that prospered for him.

CHAPTER 10

After 18 months had passed Wanda was released from rehab and eventually got back into the thick of things. Happy and full of life as she enjoyed the pleasures of home, she spent the majority of time with her son as they went everywhere together.

Doug was now back to basics and provided for their every need for he wanted to make sure she remained clean. Although he spent an enormous amount of time at home, he still managed to keep his rounds undetected. He occasionally spent nights away from home, making excuses that were legitimate. However, he was very careful in the way he moved as to avoid any more mishaps. Life was grand and they were content with the way things had turned out thus far.

Doug wondered how long it would be before Wanda started pressuring him about marriage again. Even though his intentions were good and he planned on honoring his promise, he knew he wasn't ready yet. Besides, since he was constantly meeting the most exotic females he had ever seen, and encountering the most exotic experience he had ever confronted, he wasn't ready to settle down with one woman, knowing he could have numerous women flocking around him whenever he wanted. Eventually, he knew it had to end.

Wanda sold the salon and spent her time at home caring for their son. However, that was limited as he was now in school, leaving her with too much time on her hands, which led her back to snorting cocaine. Doug never sensed it coming and remained unaware for months before catching her one night. Now his troubles were starting over again. Nevertheless, he had to get a grip on it as soon as possible. Instead of blowing up, he opted to sit and talk calmly with Wanda, convincing her to sign herself back into rehab. She thought long and hard against it. But realized it was best since she knew no other way to kick the habit. Before she entered, Doug made her promise she wouldn't leave until she regained complete control of her life. He also wanted assurance from her that quitting and staying clean was a top priority next to properly caring for their son. Their son now had knowledge of what was going on and desperately wanted her present in his life. She smiled as he kissed her before entering the establishment. Before exiting, Doug sat thinking about all the drama he had developed over the years hoping things would get better.

Mimi and Yvonne were excited, as they set the stage for the grand opening of the newly renovated nightclub elegantly named "Carolina Dymes." They had the place looking quite exquisite, as Doug would promote, they would receive mainstream exposure for the club. Also, the video show would be broadcasting live with "NAS" headlining the event. The show was well planned and surely would draw tons of attention, as other major stars would attend. Which is what they had their hearts set on as business savvy women.

Men and women alike would flock to see the show, as they would benefit from it to become owners of the number one nightclub in the state. The place was stacked with a full capacity crowd dancing and enjoying themselves as the music blared loudly. Doug started the show, as Mike worked his magic on the turntables, wasting no time giving the people what they came to see.

"The moment you have been waiting for has come. Headlining at the place to be, the magnificent Carolina Dymes nightclub, and broadcasting live, the Doug Walsh video show presents Hip Hop artist "NAS."

The thunderous roar rocked the house, as he entered on stage performing a melody of his hits and driving women crazy. Doug knew his part was done the minute he noticed the crowd in frenzy. Mimi and Yvonne walked over to thank him for giving them the exposure. They mingled through the crowd, introducing themselves and greeting friends, when suddenly they came upon three lovely women standing near the bar area.

Doug noticed Cassandra dressed lavishly, standing out amongst the crowd. Her sisters Alicia and Kiana were astonishing as well in their low cut dresses with pumps. He had no idea he would meet her at the event. However, he was thrilled at the sight of her, as fate would have it. In the midst of the five women, Doug wasted no time speaking to Cassandra as the others conversed between them, laughing.

"Hello, I see we meet again, what a coincidence," Doug stated.

"Under the circumstances, that's not such a bad thing besides, I'm really enjoying myself," she expressed.

"I'm glad you decided to come," he stated smiling.

"These are my girls, I love being around them. I wouldn't have missed it for the world," she said looking sincere.

"I wanted to speak with you the last time I saw you, but you had company for lunch," Doug implied hoping she would go into detail about who it was she had accompanying her.

"That was my husband; we are kind of separated now. However, we are still together in an odd way," she told him.

Doug didn't quite understand the significance of that statement. Therefore, he chose not to dwell on it any further, as he read between the lines thinking this was his lucky break. He took advantage of it. "So you are telling me, you are here alone," he asked cleverly.

"Not quite, these are my two sisters," she shouted above the music blasting, introducing him to Alicia and Kiana, while Mimi and Yvonne listened in curiously.

Alicia was thirty three years old, working as a lab technician at Duke Hospital. Married for ten years and separated, seeking a divorce. She was later introduced to Calvin, Doug's cousin during the event. Kiana the youngest was thirty and feisty. She was also married and employed by the department of motor vehicles in Durham, NC. She later met Mike and they all mingled in the DJ booth. NAS was on his third song when Doug continued. "What are you doing when this ends?" he whispered softly in her ear.

"Um, what you got in mind?" He came back sweetly.

"I was thinking we could go to my estate and chill while I satisfy your every desire." Doug smoothly came across.

"That's rather enticing Mr. Walsh, but how do I know if you are capable of fulfilling those needs?" she asked in a low tone.

"Because you are stressed and feeling emotional right now, which means you need to relax with the right company and in the right place at the right time. I'm sure this can be accomplished tonight with the right mindset," he assured her. Doug knew the line was lame, nevertheless, she was open game and he was going all out to obtain what he wanted.

Cassandra was already willing to take a chance. Besides, he had made it easier for her now. He was, however unaware that her intentions for being there was entirely him in the first place. "That's an interesting concept, how can I not take you up on that offer?" she responded eagerly. Suddenly, a break in the show was coming up. Doug made sure to tell Cassandra he would return shortly after she accepted his invitation.

"Sis, you are getting a little caught up over there, aren't you?" Alicia inquired, smiling at how she seemed so receptive to Doug and his advances.

"He's a gentleman," she said in a wild manner, unaware they were listening to their conversation.

They all started laughing, Kiana had made her way closer to Mike conversing, as she began feeling a connection, opening up to his advances. They hit it off well, eventually carrying it to the next stage. Calvin was straight hood, 26 years old shooting straight from the hip, no holds barred. Convincingly, he had intrigued the curiosity of Alicia tremendously in a short time with his wit and humor, someone she wasn't prone to being around, constantly drawing her closer to him. Soon, she became fascinated and intrigued by his presence.

His demeanor was challenging for a young man with a criminal record as long as his arm. Doug, as a favor, persuaded Yvonne to actually provide him employment where his criminal record wasn't an issue, never handling money. Calvin and Alicia quickly became an item, spending incredible amounts of time together in the coming weeks. After about an hour or so passed, Doug introduced "NAS" for his second set and returned to Cassandra.

"I hope that I didn't keep you waiting too long?" Doug asked.

"No, I'm fairly occupied here," she told him.

Doug had spotted Veronica in the crowd while on stage, which presented a problem. He now had to find a way to leave early. "If you get bored, we can leave anytime," he informed her. It was almost as if he read her mind, because she wasn't at all comfortable around the huge crowd and preferred being somewhere secluded and alone with him.

"That sounds good," she expressed softly.

Doug was elated she wanted to leave. He had time to close out the show to where Mimi and Yvonne could take over from. Since they had Mike to provide the music, they were set for the rest of the night. He then told Cassandra to go backstage after he closes out the broadcast, informing her where he was parked. He congratulated Yvonne and Mimi before exiting and saying goodbye to Alicia, Mike,

Kiana and Calvin.

On the deck of the estate, which was covered automatically with one-way glass from the ground up, Doug set the mood for Cassandra as he laid out some very expensive wine with the gourmet meal he had just sent over especially for the occasion. The deck of the estate had the presence of a small studio apartment which provided every comfort needed. In awe of her surroundings, she sat comfortably on the sleeping area, while soft music echoed in the background.

"Hopefully, this suits your taste and you are now relaxed and comfortable." Doug asked her.

"This is so much better, it's magnificent," she exclaimed.

"And so is this," Doug replied, moving closer, putting his arms around her and gently kissing her. Cassandra revealed how much she enjoyed it by indulging even further and sliding her hand up the thigh of his leg. Slowly teasing and rubbing his manhood. Doug eased her back on the king size bed and gently kissed her neck and caressed her breast. Rubbing his way to her mound, he discovered she wore no panties and wasted little time removing her dress and his clothes simultaneously. As he started from the neck, he made his way down her body, upon reaching her navel with his tongue, he felt her arch and tense in her back. He teased the lips of her pussy, making circling motions around them as she moaned low, feeling her desire. Cassandra opened her legs giving him access. This was new to her. However, the sensation was overwhelming. Doug then flickered gently on her clit, occasionally sucking lightly, she was moaning louder each time he circled in motion.

Then suddenly, he cupped his hands around her thighs as she lifted her legs and dove deep inside of her with his tongue finding her g-spot. She moaned loud as she tried to pull away. However, Doug was persistent and never came out, constantly circling his tongue inside to bring her to a thunderous orgasm, and tasting her juices. Cassandra lay motionless from the extent of her climax. Doug stood on his knees admiring the lovely specimen laying there. As her eyes opened, she gazed at his dick hanging low and then gently put the head in her mouth. Sucking slowly while keeping eye contact. As her motions increased, she rubbed his testicles hard arousing him enormously. Then suddenly she deep throated the length of his rod completely as he held her head.

Doug never thought she had it in her. As she vigorously sucked, he squirted in her mouth, jerking furiously. She continued until he released ever drop and then became weak. She rose and kissed him as she pushed him to the bed. While on his back, she continued sucking until he became hard again. Straddling him, she pushed down on the length of his dick until she reached the base of his pelvis and began to bounce up and down slowly, never releasing eye contact.

Doug met her motions and pulled down on her as he lifted up: bringing the intensity to greater heights and increasing her desire. He then pushed her over and got between her legs, raising them with both arms, and pushing his dick to the tilt harder and harder with each thrust. Cassandra's moans became screams as she reached orgasm. He then turned her over and lifted her up on all fours, pounding hard thrusts into her from behind. Slapping sounds echoed throughout as she hollered at each one looking back at him enjoying it. Doug eased out and pushed slowly as he tried to enter her butt, Cassandra jumped and informed him. "That's the wrong hole."

"Actually, it's the best one," he implied.

"But I can't handle that, I've never done that before," she insisted.

"I'm sure you'll like it, relax I'll be gentle," he assured her. Aware that she was against him forcefully entering her, Doug was persistent before she had time to reason. As he popped the head inside she jumped in an effort to get away. "Relax as I ease deeper," he told her.

"Don't, ah, don't put it in too deep," she informed him.

"I'll be gentle, don't worry, I won't hurt you," he said with gentle short strokes, as she slowly began to feel sensational. Although it felt like her ass was splitting, the pain felt so good. She never thought, after a few minutes of penetration, that she would or could for that matter reach an orgasm. Amazed at the effect it was having on her, she began to move in stride meeting his strokes, moaning loud as the pleasure rose. Then suddenly, Doug collapsed as he jerked uncontrollably, standing behind her. Regaining his composure, they headed to the shower. After washing one another, Cassandra grabbed his dick and started sucking it like a maniac, until it was bone hard, inserting it back in her ass again. Doug was shocked as he had never seen a woman so eager to be fucked in the ass.

Meanwhile, at the club, Yvonne met a young man that totally captured her attention. They eventually became an item as well before the end of the night and she left with the young man. Mike had made his way with Kiana and they had their fling when the night ended. However, Kiana had her sights on someone else that had caught her fancy. Constantly giving signs throughout the night, letting the individual know of her interest, she knew she would eventually get her chance since they would now see one another on a regular basis at the club. She wasn't going to be denied.

Calvin and Alicia wasted no time getting their freak on. As they left after Doug and Cassandra, Calvin fascinated her in every way, having his fill of whatever he wanted with Alicia. They fucked until the sun came up. She had completely fallen for him, and he took advantage of it.

Doug and Cassandra lay in one another's arm, talking before the sun came up. They made plans to meet again after Cassandra explained her situation concerning her husband, as Doug fully accepted the arrangement. She informed him how they spend the night in separate bedrooms among other things. He was satisfied and looking forward to spending many nights with her.

The next morning, he dropped her at the club where her car was parked and kissed her gently. Unaware that her husband was parked across the street, staring at the both of them. He had been there since the club closed waiting for her, not knowing that she wasn't there. He quickly approached, making his presence known as they stood shocked that he was there.

"What're you doing with him, I thought you were going to the club?" Her husband shouted angrily. Doug sat in awe as he waited for Cassandra to respond to the statement made by her husband and to determine if there would be some kind of confrontation.

"Excuse me? I don't answer to you since you don't have enough respect to remain loyal to me. We're separated remember or did you forget that?" she shot back angrily.

"But you're still my wife," he said bluntly.

"That's only on paper, which is about to change soon so you don't have to stalk me anymore," Cassandra yelled loudly.

Doug thought that she handled the situation well, as he noticed her husband getting back into his car leaving. "Are you going to be alright?" he asked.

"Yes! I'm going to my sister's house," she informed him.

"Call me when you get there," he told her.

"Okay, I'll see you later," she said, getting into her car. Doug waited until she pulled off before following her out of the parking lot and going their separate ways.

Kiana made it home only to find a note attached to her front door, unsigned it read: "If by chance we find each other, it's going to be beautiful." Unaware of who the note was from, she contemplated when she would interact with the individual. The next day while working, she noticed her co-worker staring as she consulted one of the patrons. Later, during her break, her co-worker approached her lightly patting her on the ass. Shocked by her openness, Kiana felt a brief sensation to the touch. She then sat beside her.

"How are you doing today?" the coworker asked.

"I'm alright, but I'm curious to know why you invited yourself to my ass?" Kiana said, smiling, hoping she would open up to break the ice since she really excited her with the advance.

Tenita White was an attractive woman with exceptional curves like an hour glass and a pretty ass. She was married with no kids, same as Kiana, and neither knew they stayed in the same neighborhood until recently. She spotted Kiana riding along and followed her.

"I couldn't resist the temptation; it looks so inviting, not to mention various other things," she said.

"And what might those things be?" Kiana asked out of curiosity.

"That's not up for discussion, I would love to show you if you are interested," Tenita shot back.

"Um, that could have its possibilities," Kiana told her.

"Good, Then I'll show you at lunch," Tenita exclaimed. Kiana was confused as to what she could possibly show her at lunch. Unaware that Tenita had it all planned. When they entered the house, Tenita told Kiana they only had thirty minutes and for her to get comfortable. Kiana now understood the comment and sat comfortably on the sofa while Tenita went into the bedroom. When she returned, Kiana noticed the strap on penis as she walked toward her naked. Her breast was firm and they bounced with each step. Her pubic hair neatly trimmed as her hip swayed. She noticed her desire reach a new height. She sat and kissed her gently. Kiana was amazed at how turned on it made her feel and eagerly matched her advance.

As she removed all her clothes, she took her to the bedroom and wasted no time indulging in some freaky wild sex. They kissed, she sucked her breast and stuck it into Kiana's mouth. She then pushed her back before making her way down her body. Kiana was so aroused she could feel her juices flowing the minute she reached her navel area. Tenita then teased the lips of her pussy. Gently sucking her clitoris and forming circles with her tongue around it. Kiana moaned loudly with pleasure building her to climax.

Suddenly, Tenita entered her with the strap on and grind slowly, as Kiana adjusted, gradually picking up the pace, pounding her pussy hard until she screamed. While climaxing, Kiana took the strap on and placed it around her before pushing it down and reversing the act. Tenita reached up and stuck the dick in her mouth, removing the juices on it. Kiana determined to see how she handled it, rolled Tenita over and pushed gently into her ass. Eagerly she accepted all she decided to give, moaning with pleasure and loving it.

They continued until she screamed her name before heading to the shower, washing and caressing one another's body. They got dressed and returned to work.

They soon became secret lovers, keeping their affair hidden from everyone. They met each other's husband and even began going out and eating dinner together. One day, Kiana's husband got sick at work, and was driven home by a coworker, after taking medication he fell asleep in the guest room unknown to Kiana. She and Tenita came in and began to satisfy one another's desires. Her husband Jim heard the noises, awakening and drowsy from the medication, he stumbled to see where it was coming from. Upon reaching the bedroom, he discovered a firm round brown ass bent over between his wife's legs. He stepped back and rubbed sleep from his eyes, and eased around looking closer as she had aroused him displaying her antics on his wife.

"That's why they're close," he thought. A show of this multitude he wasn't about to interrupt, as he watched until it was over and hurried back to the guest room. They showered, doing their normal routine, before returning to work, never knowing they were indeed a sideshow. He knew they would see each other tonight at dinner where he planned to watch them more closely.

CHAPTER 11

Calvin and Alicia were dining out, having a conversation that assured her that he was what she wanted. They had been dating now for six months. Alicia was intrigued by the way he performed sexually and how he was full of energy and very well experienced for a man of only twenty-six.

However, she wasn't aware of the other woman in his life, until the moment, a young woman walked over and shouted "You sorry bastard, I thought you were going to spend time with your son, why did you tell him a lie?" the woman yelled. Embarrassed that she confronted him in front of Alicia and letting her know about his kid, something he never mentioned, he then searched for a way to calm her down. "I'm sorry, I got caught up and couldn't make it, but I will pick him up tomorrow." Calvin told her.

"No," she said.

"What's wrong, is he sick?" Calvin asked, sounding concerned.

"If you had lived up to your obligation, you wouldn't have to ask me that, now would you?" she shot back angrily.

"Well is he?" Calvin asked, insisting she answer.

"No, I'm taking him in for a regular checkup," she informed him.

Alicia observed everything, remaining quiet as they conversed back and forth. She didn't want to get involved, aware that she wasn't going to have a choice in the matter. "I'll call you later and find out when I can come by to pick him up." Calvin expressed calmly.

"Huh, that's a joke, looks like you're spending more time with Ms. Hoochie Mama, more than your flesh and blood," she said with a nasty look. Alicia became offended even though she felt the woman had a good reason to confront Calvin about his son, even if it was in poor taste. She had no reason to disrespect her, when she never entered the conversation.

"Excuse me?" Alicia shouted angrily, while looking in the woman's direction.

"Bitch, I didn't stutter, you heard me." The woman shot back.

"Hold it, damn it, it's time for you to leave. She hasn't said a word and you took it upon yourself to insult her for no reason. Take your jealous ass home, I said I would call." Calvin expressed in anger, defending Alicia. The woman stared hard as she walked away, cursing loudly. Calvin knew that he couldn't let things get out of hand. Now he had to explain, as Alicia looked in his eyes,

"Calvin you never told me you had a son." Alicia implied.

"That's because you never asked," he told her in response.

"Is there anything else I need to know about?" she implied.

"I have two sons, by two different women, and they're both the same way, lots of jealousy and drama all the time," he informed her.

"So you're telling me that this is constant?" she asked.

"I'm telling you, it's something I've been dealing with since we departed, and I have no control over it, which is why I'm no longer with either of them," he explained.

"I'm sorry, it's just that I don't understand it," she exclaimed openly.

"Well, it's obvious you weren't brought up in the hood," he shot back. Alicia tried not being offended by his statement, even though she knew he was being sarcastic, implicating the depth of her blackness. However, she knew better and came back at him hard.

"I have to say you're right. I was brought up to respect others with my mannerism, unlike the majority of our race, who has no sense of direction," she stated firmly. The waitress approached with their food. Calvin was happy that she did as he wanted to change the subject anyway. They continued conversing as they ate. Alicia was concerned about the amount of attention that Calvin gave the woman. She thought of ways to persuade him to devote his attention to her and control the way he interacts with others. Calvin felt his sense of control in the conversation. He never entertained the thought to discuss the issue with her, instead he would find ways to change the subject. Nevertheless, Calvin had no intentions of putting her up on a pedestal by any means; he was a free spirited individual.

Dealing with the opposite attraction became a challenge for them both. As Alicia was a straight forward, abiding, well-mannered citizen. Calvin was, on the other hand, totally different. Constantly out to make a dollar, doing whatever it takes in every aspect of his life and others, even if he had to exploit someone else to achieve what he wanted.

Meanwhile, Yvonne bought a BMW and had it financed through the bank in her name and presented it to her companion. Things really took off as they went everywhere together. This, however, only lasted for a short while before she started seeing him less and less on a daily basis. It seemed as though she had to make an appointment to see him.

Yvonne became outraged at the thought of his behavior and wanted to take the car away from him to prevent him from spending so much time away from her. Instead, she reasoned otherwise, patiently hoping and expecting a change. However, it only seemed to get worse as time went along. Yvonne and Mimi prepared for the New Year's night party. They contemplated on how many people might attend, having no absolute idea what kind of crowd they might draw tonight, when suddenly, Yvonne noticed Michael pull into the parking lot with others in the car. As they exit, she noticed the passengers are Calvin, Alicia and Kiana, ready to bring in the New Year with a bang, as they were elegantly dressed for the occasion. There were loads of people standing- up in line to attend, as they wanted to see the headliner.

"I see y'all got things in order baby." Michael told Yvonne.

"Mimi is a perfectionist, everything must be to her liking. Which means I work hard to make sure it's correct besides, it's about to be "1999" in a couple of hours," she said.

"Have you made any resolutions?" he asked her, smiling,

"Would you believe I have?" she shot back, hoping she could get her point across, throwing hints at what she wanted from him in the relationship.

"What are they?" he asked in response.

"I have decided to devote my time and undivided attention to my man and make his desires; hopes and dreams become reality so that we're content and happy forever," she stated, looking serious, while staring into the depths of his soul. Michael knew exactly what she meant by the statement.

"Sometimes you have to be careful what you ask for because you just might get it. However, we're often unable to see what it is we are after, when it's right there before us," he stated, somewhat giving her the indication he understood her. But thought otherwise about fulfilling what she wanted out of him.

The night of New Year's Eve brought out a host of people that normally wouldn't attend any other night at the club. This night was special to everyone and they took advantage of the event, having fun as they partied all night long. As the night went on, Yvonne would occasionally notice Michael engaging in conversation with various women. She dismissed the obvious and continued to make sure that everyone enjoyed themselves, when Calvin pulled her onto the dance floor, forcing her to loosen up and get into the mix.

Suddenly the music ended and she attempted to go back to the bar, as Calvin wrapped his arms around her for her to continue dancing. The sound of Luther Vandross blasted through the club and slowed the mood. As they slow danced, Calvin felt that he had to reveal something to Yvonne concerning Michael, but he did not want to impose the wrong way. However, he felt she deserved the right to know anyway.

"How are things with you and Michael?" he asked her, as he noticed Michael watching them closely from a distance.

"They're going, pretty good," she said hesitantly.

"I see y'all spending a lot of time together," he remarked, knowing that was a lie.

"Actually, we don't spend that much time together," she replied.

"I wonder why? With a woman of your charm and intellect, I would cherish you," he stated honestly,

"Really, Calvin?" Yvonne replied, blushing, astonished and honored by the comment.

"I guess he spends too much time elsewhere." Calvin shot back.

"Now what does that mean?" she asked concerned.

"I mean I wouldn't be doing those things," he told her.

"Is there by any chance you know something that I don't, because if you do, I would appreciate you telling me," she implied.

"Well, you didn't hear it from me, but Michael has been spending an incredible amount of time around the trailer park," he said.

"Doing what Calvin?" she asked frankly.

"He's seeing this white girl named Liza Sizemore, she has him fascinated or something, he can't stay away from her."

Yvonne stopped as her anger rose. She looked at Calvin. "Are you absolutely certain about this?" she asked, looking in his eyes.

"I've been there, of course I'm certain, you think I talk for conversation? Bank on it," he said, grabbing her attention. She turned to walk away and noticed Mimi standing near the bar with Mike and

Kiana, laughing. As she joined them, Mike headed for the booth to mix some more sound, as the dance floor remained crowded.

"I see you're having a ball out there dancing." Mimi stated.

"I was until, never mind," she said looking away. Mimi and Kiana sensed something was wrong, observing one another as Yvonne walked towards Michael.

"I wonder what's wrong with her." Mimi implied.

"She needs loving, what else could it be?" Kiana responded.

"I hate seeing her in that state, I wish I could help her, she's my best friend," she said in a mild tone.

"Do you always care so deeply for your friends?" Kiana asked with intentions of taking the conversation to a new depth.

"When they're good to me," she replied back.

"I could be good to you in more ways than you can imagine. If you give me the chance," Kiana stated with a smile. Although Mimi was a bit uncomfortable, she never swayed from the question and decided to open up a little further.

"And how far do you think we could go?" she asked.

"As far as you like, considering your limits," Kiana replied. Mimi led Kiana into the office area and closed the door; Kiana cupped her firm tight ass tightly, kissing her intensely while making eye contact. She then lowered herself down, reaching her skirt. She pulled her panties down to reveal the perfectly trimmed pubic hairs, surrounding the lips of her pussy. She gently licked around the edges before teasing her clitoris.

This made Mimi tense up, grabbed her head and shoved it into the mound of her pussy, hard. Kiana felt the sensation she had on her indulged her tongue faster and harder as she moaned in pleasure, until a burst of passion erupted as she got weaker standing. They moved in front of the desk. Kiana removed her clothes and lay down onto the carpet, inviting Mimi to join her. She then straddled her head laying her body down until she felt wet, hot lips touching her pussy. They continuously teased one another into oblivion as they performed the most intense oral sex, arousing each other to climax over and over; enjoying it tremendously together. Suddenly, they heard the door knob turn, however, it was locked. They jumped up to hurry and get clothed. As they turned, Yvonne stepped in, turned the lights and observed Kiana buttoning her blouse.

"I didn't know y'all were in here," Yvonne responded. Shocked that she had interrupted them and somewhat embarrassed a bit.

"We decided to come take a break and it just escalated a bit, but hopefully this will not leave this room," she asked.

"Girl, you know my lips are sealed." Yvonne assured her, confused as she never thought Mimi was a lesbian. However, she already knew about Kiana as that was no secret. Everyone knew she was freaky and outspoken. They joined everyone having fun as if nothing happened. Yvonne only came to the office to avoid Mike and his corny advances toward her, having little knowledge that Yvonne wasn't the least bit interested in him. But that didn't stop him as he constantly pursued her.

Meanwhile, Alicia ran around looking for Calvin when she noticed his baby's mama in the club. Upon finding him wrapped up in another woman in the corner, she stood silently watching, unnoticed by them as they caressed one another. She could not put up with his behavior and disrespect and decided to confront him at the proper time instead of causing a scene. She walked away, heading for the bar and took a seat.

"Hello, I've never seen you here before?" The gentleman stated.

"I don't come out much, but I've been here a few times. Do you come here often?" she asked in response.

"Actually, I've never been here, that was my way of breaking the ice to start a conversation," he said laughing.

"Well, I must say you accomplished your task. It worked," she said, smiling as she noticed his attractiveness.

"My name is Mickey. Mickey Douglas," he told her.

"Hi, I'm Alicia Blackman, pleased to make your acquaintance," she expressed.

"Can I offer you a drink?" he asked politely.

"That would be nice," she said kindly. After talking for what seemed to be hours, they began laughing as they were both tipsy, enjoying themselves.

"Are you here alone?" he asked.

"No, but it seems like my date is occupied elsewhere," she told him.

"That's his fault, because he's going to miss this," he implied.

"Miss what?" Alicia replied, failing to understand as to what he was implying. He then grabbed her by the arm leading her to his car. She did not resist for once. Instead, she opted to look and see who might have seen her. They arrived at the Marriott Hotel and entered the bar.

"The atmosphere is pleasant and quiet," he informed her. Alicia couldn't believe she was attracted to this total stranger, and was led off into the night. But thus far, she was thrilled to be in such good company. They made it to his room and watched a movie. As Alicia got comfortable Mickey moved closer, putting his arms around and kissing her softly. Noticing no resistance, he caressed her breast firmly, feeling the hardening of her nipples.

He gently removed her top and skirt, revealing her luscious body wrapped in silk undergarments. After removing her brand panties, he then commenced to arousing her extremely, kissing her neck, breast, navel and around the mound of her pussy, as if she was a delicacy. Alicia was being pleasured with every touch from this complete stranger and loving it, moaning out loud. He penetrated her with rugged thrusts, deeper and deeper while looking into her eyes and watching her reactions. She climaxed instantly, holding him tightly, jerking uncontrollably.

This aroused her even more, as she lifted her legs up and gave him access to reach deep within her and explore. Mickey drove all he had in her pounding hard as she screamed his name louder and louder. Suddenly he erupted, squirting his load in her before collapsing on top of her, breathing hard. Both were satisfied. However, Alicia couldn't believe she had met a total stranger and became intimate within 2 hours. They showered and got dressed before midnight. They had time to make it back to the club, and watch the ball drop, bringing in the New Year.

12:00 midnight; the ball drops as they watch the confetti flying everywhere and everyone hollering "Happy New Year."

The place was ecstatic as Prince blasted through the speakers; "Party like it's 1999" played over the course of twenty minutes. Mike had remixed the cut and added some flavor to it. The night everyone had been waiting for came to a close with a big bang. Meanwhile, Cassandra and Doug sat together enjoying their New Year in bed, watching television. Neither of them wanted to go out and celebrate with a crowd, they preferred being alone as they enjoyed one another, making love constantly through the night, resting only to talk about their future.

Doug was falling deeply in love with Cassandra, but he never forgot his promise to Wanda. Nevertheless, his emotions were beginning to control his thoughts, which were focused solely on Cassandra, as she surrendered to his every desire, fully fulfilling his needs. Something he hadn't experienced with no other woman in his life before. At least he had plenty of time to enjoy himself, knowing it would be another 18 months before Wanda would return from rehab. Therefore, he saw no reason not to enjoy himself.

Prior to everyone going out on New Year's Eve, Kiana never considered why her husband preferred to stay home alone. She was unaware that her lover and coworker would lie naked in her man's arms while she celebrated New Year's at the club.

"That was nice," she said as she slowly removed his dick.

"And you're great yourself," he said, looking at her smiling. She slid her hand down until she reached his dick, lying semi hard and began sucking in slow motion, putting the head of his dick between her teeth, playfully biting down on it while looking directly into his face. They now had their little secret that they agreed never to reveal to Kiana and her husband.

However, they hoped they could continue seeing each other without being detected by either one of them. It could remain part of their weekly routine since his wife never paid much attention to anything he did and her husband rarely fucked her anymore. Therefore, they had planned it well and continued being intimate without Kiana or her husband ever noticing anything unusual.

"Do you know what excited me about you?" he asked.

"I'm really curious to find out," she replied quickly.

"The moment I saw you and Kiana make out, it brought my desire to a level I couldn't control and I wasn't about to interrupt before I watched it all."

"Did you really enjoy it?" she asked interested.

"More than you'll ever imagine," he responded.

"Then we shouldn't get bored with each other," she implied.

"I don't see that happening," he said quickly rubbing her ass.

Tenita was elated because she had the best of both worlds. She wasn't getting the satisfaction from her husband, but Kiana and her husband filled the void, and she liked the arrangement, the way it was now.

On the other side of town, Yvonne was growing tired of Michael and his antics. After discussing his actions at the club, the various women she found out about only added fuel to the fire. He denied everything as if he was really being truthful. However, after being informed by Calvin, she was now on the edge and contemplating taking the car back. Calvin told her that he did have someone to help her, providing that she handles the finances for it. Yvonne agreed as he had his friend Tim contact her. After giving him the info and telling him to remain light, they later met up at the trailer park. Yvonne had found out they were out of town and easily spotted the car.

"Hi, you must be Yvonne?" he said, smiling as he adored the lovely lady before him.

"And you're Tim?" she responded back. Noticing that young man looked to be about 18 years old, she wanted this to be done as quickly as possible, being she wasn't at all comfortable in his company, especially after she spotted the bulge underneath his shirt. After explaining what she was about to do, she informed him that he would drive the car and he was to follow her in her car. He agreed as Yvonne stipulated she would give him one hundred dollars and he had to make it home from there. She got in the car and sped off, thinking she had to have some place he couldn't find it. Then it hit her, Doug.

"Hello," Doug answered.

"Doug, this is Yvonne, I need your help," she said quickly.

"Sure, what is it?" he asked.

"I need to store my car until I can sell it," she exclaimed.

"No problem, bring it over," he told her.

"I'm on my way, thanks," she replied happily.

"I'll be here," he shot back. She then headed towards the estate, where she arrived about 20 minutes later. She then exited the BMW, retrieved the money from her pocket and handed it through the window to Tim. She informed him she would handle things from here. Tim exited the car and started walking, as he grabbed his cell phone and dialed someone to pick him up. He was curious about who occupied the estate, but thought about Calvin reminding him to remain light.

Doug exited and drove the BMW into his garage, parking it beside a host of other expensive cars. Yvonne thanked him and explained the situation to Doug, who was humble to her needs. He told her that she could always lean on him for whatever she needed, assuring her that he considered her a very dear friend. In a matter of minutes, they discussed how things were going with Cassandra being the main focus of the conversation, before she departed and headed home. While driving down the street, she decided to pull into the convenience store. She spotted Tim inside and figured that he had walked this far since he left.

"Hey, you caught up with me," he told her joking.

"I thought I saw you call someone?" she shot back.

"I did, but they haven't shown up," he told her.

"I guess I could give you a ride." Yvonne told him, figuring that's the least she could do for him since he helped her. They exited the store after purchasing their drinks. While drinking, Tim remained quiet until he noticed she was uneasy.

"If it's not too personal, what are you going to do with that car?" Tim asked curiously.

"Sell it, why are you interested?" she asked.

"I might be able to help you," he informed her.

"Really?" she shot back.

"Of course, as a matter of fact, I'm headed there now if you have time. You can talk to him yourself," he told her. Yvonne thought hard about the encounter in such a rough neighborhood, but reasoned, what could it hurt? She met his friend as they pulled up at this nicely manicured lawn that a very nice split level home adorned for this neighborhood. After Tim told his friend about Yvonne and the car, he approached the car slowly. Yvonne had been watching closely, observing everything and her surroundings while sitting there. Soon, her attention became focused on the young man headed her way.

"Hello, I'm Shadow, Tim tells me you have a nice BMW for sale?" he asked her with a mild demeanor.

Yvonne appeared stunned as she regrouped and confirmed that was correct. "Yes!" She said hesitantly. After discussing the details of the car, Shadow told her he would have to see it before he could agree to her price out of the blue. However, they made the agreement in the following days and amazingly became friends. Shadow purchased the car for $32,000 cash, something Yvonne wasn't in agreement with but found a way to cover it up at the bank. During the time they became friends, Shadow would often listen as Yvonne explained her situation to him, she felt at ease talking and confiding in him, eventually telling him how she keeps getting phone calls from Michael pertaining to her taking the car back and selling it.

They began going out sometimes and he began to frequent the club occasionally, learning her lifestyle. They grew closer as time went by and she got to know his mother, whom she happened to click well with first time they met. After Shadow got to know about her business ventures, he encouraged her in every way. Upon finding out about her desire to own and operate her own publishing company, he quickly engaged the thought of his mother, who had her own inspiration regarding the same ventures.

As he thought about his brother Marquis, who was locked up in prison, who loved to write and had already started putting the finishing touches on a couple of projects that he had written earlier in there, Shadow thought it would be a good idea to introduce her to him and see if they could help each other. His plan was already instilled in him by Marquis, since he always expressed how he wanted to write books and form a publishing company of his own. Shadow ran with the idea and convinced his mother and Yvonne to form "Gatehouse Publications." Once Shadow received a collect call from Marquis and explained the situation, Marquis was grateful and eager to meet her over the phone.

"Hello," the voice answered softly.

"Hello Yvonne, this is Marquis, Shadow's brother," he said.

"Hi, I'm glad to meet you, I've heard quite a lot about you, especially concerning your interest in writing," she exclaimed.

"I've got quite a few books completed and numerous ideas and thoughts for other projects," he told her. As they made small talk, feeling one another out, they began to get a sense of connection started where they became somewhat comfortable expressing parts of themselves to each other.

Marquis then decided to see where her mental state resided. "Yvonne, you seem as though you're an intelligent individual, can I ask you a question?" he inquired.

"Sure," she replied.

"What would you do if you had access to a $100,000?" he asked.

"Well, that's not a lot of money, however, I do see some things I could acquire and make it yield more," she told him.

"What, for instance?" he inquired, hoping she would elaborate a bit further to give him a sense of where she was mentally.

"Small investments where its little risk, like real estate or in my club," she stated.

Marquis thought that was a logical answer and inquired further. "So how do you view friendship?" he asked calmly.

"Depends on how in depth they become. I give what I feel is appropriate to how I'm treated," she replied.

"Do you agree that honesty and truth is the best policy?" he asked.

"That's a good concept to build the foundation on," she insisted agreeing.

"Based on the assumption you and I were on those terms, would there be any limitations?" he asked.

"Actually, I feel as though you should remain sincere in every aspect of the relationship. If it's to serve any purpose and have any meaning, or you defeat the purpose of being together," she shot back.

"I find it hard to put my complete trust in anyone, being I always regret it in the end," he exclaimed.

"Maybe you need to learn how to trust in yourself first, and then you might discern how to better trust in others," she told him.

"So how does that relate to you?" he asked her.

"Basically, it's how I interact," she exclaimed.

"So it's safe to say, I can trust you?" he asked in return.

"Well, you hardly know me, but on the contrary, yes!" She expressed.

"That's interesting to know," he came back.

"I'm curious, why do you ask?" she said.

"Because before I got caught up in this mess, I had a lump sum of money and now I'm having a hard time finding someone to trust that can retrieve it for me," he informed her.

"What about your family, mother, or brother?" she asked him.

"I can't put my mom in that predicament, and I can't rely on my brother under the circumstances," he informed her.

"Both of them, huh, but you're willing to trust me somewhat, of a total stranger?" she told him.

"Aren't you trustworthy?" he asked.

"Yes, but why me?" she replied.

"Because I feel a certain vibe within that puts me at ease with you and my instincts tell me that I'm right." Marquis informed her.

"Therefore, you want me to do it for you?" she asked.

"Yes, but I'm still not sure if you're capable either, because of where I stashed it, which makes it complex for even you. However, we'll just see how it plays out," he informed her.

As time went on they shared their hopes and dreams, through phone conversations and casual visits. They constantly confided in one another as they focused on their business venture together. They had high hopes of creating and managing a successful publishing company, which could lead to various other things. As they became productive together, they made progress slowly, but only time would tell their fate.

CHAPTER 12

On the morning of September 3, 1999, Doug received a devastating phone call. He had been informed that his Auntie Ruth had been in a car accident, and arrived at the hospital D.O.A. Now he had lost someone else close to him, which he couldn't replace, and this only made matters worse. Depressed and feeling sorry for himself, he began to drink heavily as the phone rings.

"Hello," he answered.

"Doug, are you alright?" Cassandra asked concerned.

"I'm maintaining," he said. However, she sensed that was a lie from the sound of his voice, being she had come to know him well.

"I'm coming over, you are not going anywhere are you?" Cassandra said.

"No, I'll be here," he told her.

"Alright, I'll be there in a few minutes," she exclaimed, knowing he needed comforting and help in making arrangements. She wanted to be there for him in every way. In the midst of his loss, friends from all over came to console him and by midday the house was full. The arrangements were made for the burial.

Doug and Cassandra arranged the wake for Saturday at the estate, with the lavish funeral set for Sunday. They all managed to carry on through the week, contemplating the effects of the weekend, where things were sure to become more hectic.

The estate was crowded with friends and family members. Some of them from out of town, Doug never knew.

"How're you making it Mr. Walsh?" Michelle asked as everyone listened.

"I'm doing fine, thank you for coming," he responded.

"I'm always here for you," Michelle shot back.

Noticing their conversation Cassandra moved closer. "Baby, you want a drink?" Cassandra asked intentionally interrupting their conversation.

"That would be nice Cassandra," Doug said smiling.

"Hello, how are you?" Cassandra replied.

"Fine, I'm glad to meet you," she responded. As Cassandra went to fix Doug a drink, Michelle looked her up and down as if she had no business there. Unaware that she too was being watched in the same manner, as Yvonne sat observing everything. Calvin and Alicia walked in late, along with Kiana and her husband, who also brought their friends aka lover Tenita and her husband. They all instantly mingled and got cozy with the guest quickly. Rita observed everyone while staying a distance from Doug. Hiding her anger, as she hated the fact that her relationship wasn't open like his and Cassandra's. However, that wasn't going to stop her from making her presence known by any means.

"Hi Doug," Rita expressed as she walked up to him, while standing and talking to Michelle.

"Hello Rita, it's nice you could make it," he responded, hoping she wouldn't make a scene, being that he had several women there that he was intimately involved with.

"I had to come and give my condolences," she replied.

"Thank you, I'm very grateful," he shot back.

"If you got time later, I would like to discuss business, that could become very prosperous for us both." Doug knew exactly what she meant and quickly dismissed it.

"I'm not up to discussing anything right now, however, I will get back to you soon," he responded. Suddenly Cassandra returned with his drink. Rita felt as though he was avoiding her, as he had been doing that a lot lately. Now she was beginning to see the reason why. Mike decided to take the sadness out of the room by setting the radio on some smooth jazz. Doug walked to the terrace where he encountered Veronica talking with Kiana and her husband.

"This is a very nice view, I would love to live here, it's really pleasant." Veronica stated while looking at Doug. He wondered why she hadn't gotten the chance to see it before now.

"Thank you, it has its possibilities," he informed her. Kiana being very observant noticed the gleam in the eyes of Veronica while she was talking to Doug.

"Can you give me a tour of the place?" she asked him hoping to get him alone.

"Now?" he shot back, knowing her intentions.

"This is as good a time as any," she replied. As they headed off, Kiana let her curiosity get the best of her, she knew something wasn't right. As Doug and Veronica came to the patio, she turned and kissed him, passionately while rubbing his manhood. Doug obliged and cupped her ass tightly. He wasted no time pulling her panties off. Easing her on the bed, he penetrated her deeply, thrusting hard as she raised her legs giving him full access to the gold mine in her pussy. When suddenly, Kiana walked in and watches the action unnoticed and walks around the bed. Doug stopped, shocked he was caught and at the sight of who it was. Not to mention how luscious she looked standing there. Her firm breast were erect and her pretty round brown ass was plump.

"Is three a crowd?" she asked, looking at Doug and rubbing her neatly trimmed mound while licking her lips.

"Not at all, " Veronica responded before Doug spoke. Kiana went behind Doug while he was deep in Veronica and began sucking his nuts, as she played with Veronica's clit. She then pulled his dick out of her pussy and sucked furiously until she drained him, forcing him to release his load in her mouth. Veronica became excited watching her work. Kiana then grabbed her legs and buried her face into her pussy while giving Doug access to back door her.

Tempted by the pretty brown round in his face, he entered her and slowly penetrated with long strokes, as she moaned and continuously teased Veronica, bringing her to climax. Doug became excited and quickened his strokes until his dick accidentally slipped out. Kiana reached around, grabbed it and put it into the hilt. As she gasped loudly for air, he stroked her pretty ass until he shot his load far. They hurried and cleaned up before anyone noticed their absence and returned to the den area as if nothing happened.

"That was nice, we must do this again," Kiana said smiling.

"I'm looking forward to it," Veronica responded.

"What about you Doug, did you enjoy it?" Kiana asked him.

"As much as I hate to say it, Yes! But I'm feeling guilty about your sister," he replied.

"Don't worry, what she doesn't know won't hurt her. Besides, I'm not telling her anyway, shit she is lucky to have you the way you pushed that dick up in me." Kiana said laughing.

Little did they know Michelle was also watching in the cut and furious as hell. Now she not only had to deal with Cassandra, but her sister as well and this other bitch. She wasted no time confronting Doug when she got him alone.

"Did you have fun?" she asked nonchalantly.

"What?" he asked, unaware of what she meant.

"Did those two whores satisfy you?" she shot back furiously.

"I haven't the slightest idea what you are talking about," he responded.

"Don't give me that, I saw you," she stated.

"Since when do I answer to you?" Doug shot back angrily.

"It's just that I care and I don't think you should be involved with these women and I don't think Cassandra would appreciate this either," she expressed harshly.

"Now you are threatening me?" he asked angrily.

"That's not a threat, it was only a thought," she replied.

"Well, here is a thought for you, get the hell out of my house and stay the hell out of my house right now." Doug said furiously.

Michelle realized that he said this out of anger and didn't want to agitate him any further. "I'm sorry, I'll leave and I'll see you Monday," she stated softly.

"Don't bother; your services are no longer needed at the office either. Hopefully you won't have a problem finding employment." Doug told her in a harsh tone. Michelle broke down in tears as she realized she had gone too far. But she wasn't going to go without a fight.

Doug conversed with family, friends and their guests until the wake was over. After everyone left, Cassandra cleaned up and made sure he was comfortable.

"Baby I realize you're depressed, if you want to be alone, I'll leave," she informed him.

"Thanks for your consideration, but I prefer your company. I love you and there's no one else I would want to be here with me right now, if you don't mind," he told her.

"I must say I'm honored," she responded.

"Good, let's go to bed, I'm... you know," he said muttering.

"Did you say what I think you said?" she asked.

"Evidently, your mind is in the gutter," he responded humorously.

"We'll see about that Mr," she replied back. Doug then led her to the bedroom and made passionate love to her. With the antics he had learned over the years, he brought her to the most powerful climaxes she had ever experienced.

"Where do we go from here?" he asked, holding her tightly realizing she had become a major impact in his life. Cassandra looked into his eyes gazing brightly thinking of how she could explain that she had no intentions of ever leaving her husband, even though they were not on good terms.

"Only time can answer that question," she responded and turned over on top of him as if she was going to sleep.

After the funeral, Doug felt the cold stare from Michelle and thought he may have been too harsh. But he couldn't let her impose on his personal life. And he had to set the standard even though he was intimately involved with her also. Once everyone departed, he chose to stay at the burial sight and meditate by himself.

"Auntie I miss you. I know I never told you, but I'm sure you know. I love you, rest in peace." Suddenly, Yvonne walked up and grabbed his hand to console him that everything will be alright. "I thought you left?" he said softly.

"I did until I realized you might need someone to talk to other than your aunt. Someone to give you an honest answer," she said.

"I have always been confident in confiding in you," he told her.

"I felt the same way also, which is why I came back to talk to you," she responded. "I've been going through some things for a while as you already know: the drama with my husband messing around, using my son against me, and then my so called boyfriend who turned out to be a zero," she said.

"I must say you have had a rough ride," Doug said.

"Now I've met a man that's in prison with a life sentence. He has potential, to mention various other talents. And we are trying to accomplish the task of developing a publishing company together; he's already completed a couple of urban books. And has a guy helping him on the inside; creating more interesting projects that's rather intriguing. However, I'm afraid to give him my undivided attention in fear of my doubts. And this basically eliminates any chance we have of getting it off of the ground, so I'm asking your opinion in regards to it," she stated honestly.

"Yvonne most people won't see a future there because they're limited in their possibilities and often confused with their thought, not knowing if they will ever return to society. Nelson Mandela was a prime example, he spent 27 years behind bars, only to return home and become productive again. Nevertheless, it's not about what others say or think, it's about what you feel within you, and whether or not this man has your best interest at heart.

Everything happens for a reason and we can be motivated by only certain people that actually touches our inner being, regardless of whether we've known them or not. And in no time, we grow attached to a certain part of the individual that comforts and moves us in ways others we loved haven't. To the point we start thinking of them often. Although our fears and doubts remain at the surface, the reality of it can never be dismissed because the possibility will always exist. So never say never, because later on you may look back only to say what if, then it's too late," he said.

"I can't believe you actually read me, because I do have my doubts and fear sets in constantly in every aspect. Upon first reading his first book, I sensed how well he writes, although I became bored with certain parts and disagreed with some of the dialogue," she said.

"Therefore, you liked his work?" Doug asked.

"Yes!" she responded.

"So if you were in his shoes, would you send me your best work first?" Doug asked.

"I never thought of it in those terms," she replied back.

"That's because you are limited in your possibilities and you are not open minded to think positive about someone in a negative atmosphere. All he has time to do is think and produce positive results, basically because he's already at his lowest point in life. Where else is it for him to go but up, unless he chose to die," Doug responded seriously.

"I would never come to that conclusion," she said softly.

"Because you're only seeing what's presented in front of you. But once you remove the blinders, you'll see the big picture and be more prone to do whatever it takes to produce what's yours for the taking," he told her.

"So you're saying I need to open-up?" she asked.

"Not at all. I'm only saying, you need to stay focused and only retrieve what's being presented to you without fear and doubt dictating your life for you, or you'll never achieve your goals and release your own potentials. You have what it takes, don't be scared to take a chance. That's what life's all about Yvonne. Choices and chances, that's what God gave us so use them," he expressed hugging her as they walked from the grave site.

"I'm so comfortable talking to you," she told him.

"I guess that's why we're such good friends, huh?" Doug replied.

"Thank you for being so understanding. You made things so much easier for me, because I have been dwelling on this for quite some time," she told him.

"Hopefully you see things in the proper perspective and eventually it will all come together for you." Doug stated.

"I sure hope so," she exclaimed.

"Who knows, he might become your soul mate." Doug told her. They looked at one another laughing as he closed the door to her car, sending her off. He then noticed someone standing afar on the hill of the cemetery watching them. But couldn't make out who it was, male or female. He got into his car, following Yvonne as she headed to the entrance. He wanted to go see who the individual was that was watching them, but dismissed the thought deciding to go visit Veronica instead. Being he had been overwhelmed the night before with their sexual escapade.

Doug arrived at the townhouse complex and noticed an enormous amount of cars parked in the lot which was very unusual. As he entered, he heard music blasting and made his way down the hall only to see Veronica and Kiana in the bedroom. Unaware of his presence, he watched as Veronica buried her face into the mound of Kiana's pussy. She moaned loudly, squeezing her breast until her nipples became erect.

Doug walked in behind Veronica. Kiana eyes popped wide open as she noticed they were no longer alone. He undressed and lay beside her, caressing her breasts while Veronica continued licking her clit. Aroused by the sensitive touch of his hand, she reached down and began stroking his dick until it became rock hard. Noticing his hardness, Veronica rose up and put it in her mouth sucking it furiously. Kiana straddled his head and lowered herself down upon his face as Doug sucked on the mound of her pussy.

Suddenly, he erupted squirting his juices in Veronica's mouth, as she eagerly swallowed every drop while looking at him sucking Kiana's pussy. She then stroked hard; bringing his dick erect again and straddling him as she slowly eased down until she reached the base of his penis. Then began to ride furiously, controlling the tempo, bringing herself to climax over and over. Kiana, on the other hand, fought hard to stay balanced upon his face, holding on as the intensity of Doug's tongue drove her into a frenzy. Suddenly a loud click noise popped startling Doug and Kiana. They both collapsed on the bed totally exhausted.

"What was that noise?" Doug asked curiously.

"The air conditioning unit." Neither one of them had any idea they were being recorded and the video sold for a nice profit. Veronica was making a tremendous amount of money selling her videotapes and photos overseas and on the internet. This one would bring top dollar as they thrive for threesomes more than anything and she intended to give them all she could. Now she had to put the final touches on it.

She then began sucking hard on Doug's dick to get it good and erect. As she motioned for Kiana to straddle him, she inserted it into her ass and began licking his balls. She knew this would excite him to explode quickly. Gradually she licked around the base of his dick, easing her way to Kiana's pussy arousing her even more while Doug penetrated her ass. The camera had a direct shot of each one of them as they performed the most erotic sex on each other. Kiana screamed as an enormous climax racked her intensely before Doug erupted his load in her ass. They all showered together, washing each other's body and using their antics to further satisfy their desires. Later on, they ate and watched television while talking about the sex they had.

CHAPTER 13

Michelle felt she had things under control, but now it seemed that things were slipping away from her and getting out of hand. She knew she had to take drastic measures quickly. So she phoned the bank and had the controlling interest of the newly acquired office buildings transferred to a bogus real estate firm in her name. This way she could easily post a sell without being detected by anyone in Doug's firm (at least that's what she thought.)

However, she wasn't aware that Yvonne had already begun making arrangements for all of Doug's assets to come through her. Therefore, she had to authorize anything involved in his firm, giving her firsthand knowledge of everything. Upon finding out about this, she blocked the transaction, then later informed Doug of what Michelle was trying to do and improvised a plan to acquire the property from her. Doug was furious at the thought of Michelle trying to actually take half a million dollars from under his nose.

Nevertheless, she had to be taught a valuable lesson about crossing someone that had graciously been good to her. However, he had to do it the right way because there were many people who knew about him firing her at the wake. Therefore, violence wasn't an option concerning her without anyone becoming suspicious. Hopefully, he could prevent her from accomplishing her mission, by threatening her in another way.

Michelle had filed a complaint with the EEOC (Equal Employment Opportunity Commission), in regards to her being fired, and claiming the grounds for her termination were inappropriate. She then filed a civil suit for sexual harassment, hoping this would convince Doug to reconsider dismissing her. However, none of it fazed Doug. It only made him harden his heart, that much more and refusing to take any of her calls or speak to her in public. He already had another plan to make her see things in another way that he was sure to get her attention.

Meanwhile, Wanda was making incredible progress improvising with all she had available to her. She was spending most of her time on the computer after classes, something she always cherished at home, when she came across photos of Doug with some mysterious woman. She became furious that he had betrayed her. Unable to make contact with the outside world, she had to conjure up a way to get in touch with him again, ASAP.

Knowing that she had another three months before she completed the program, there was no way she could wait that long. However, there was a fax machine in the main office, if she could get to it, she could get a message to Doug. Only one guard stood in her way, she needed a plan quickly. "Rhonda, I need your help girl," she told her friend. Wanda figured since she helped Rhonda cope with her problems since the day she got there, that was the least she could do to repay her, being that she had a thing for the guard anyway.

"What is it?" she responded.

"I need to get into the front office and send out a fax. Therefore, I need you to distract the guard for me and I mean keep him busy for at least five minutes," she responded happily. Wanda knew she was going to put on a show and desperately wanted to see it. But she had business to tend to.

As she got ready to sneak into the office, Rhonda went to work. She pranced down the hall, knowing everyone was asleep and stepped around the corner, letting her nightgown pop open for the guard to see her nipples and the pubic hair on her pussy. She hoped that would entice him into her room. She motioned to him with one hand, while the other caressed her breast and winked at him seductively. He followed her quickly into the room, where she wasted no time unbuttoning his pants and retrieving his dick in her mouth, sucking furiously while he guided her with his hand. She then laid on the edge of the bed and held her legs high, exposing her pussy, inviting him graciously.

Ready and willing to oblige her, he mounted her, stroking fast and hard until he exploded. Rhonda knew she had to contain him a few more minutes longer so she grabbed his dick and stroked hard before she sucked him dry. Regaining his composure, she had him rock hard all over again, his knees were getting weak as she drained the life out of him. Then suddenly Rhonda saw Wanda at the door, peeking in on them. She quickly increased her motion, forcing him to explode once again as he quickly came into her mouth. He then pulled up his pants, and informed Rhonda of how much he appreciated it and not to hesitate asking if she needed anything, before he left to go back to his post. Wanda came in laughing out loud.

"Girl, when I saw his face, I almost died, you had him going crazy," she told her laughing.

"I know, he was trembling the whole time," she shot back.

"Thanks, I needed that." Wanda responded.

"You know I got your back, you're my girl, plus he said if I need anything, don't hesitate to ask."

"You go girl, we might need him again, keep it hot on that ass." Wanda responded.

"Did you do what you had to do?" she asked Wanda.

"Of course and you gave me plenty of time," she responded.

"Good! Now let's get something to eat, that nigga got me hungry and I need to take a shower before I go to bed," she replied.

"My treat girl, get anything you want out of my box." They ate and talked about the fax she sent along with other things as they had become close friends. Wanda had become very fond of Rhonda.

Rhonda was a Caucasian that everyone else looked down on in the program, because of her upbringing. She came from a very rich family, leading them to think she had no business there in the first place. Jealousy and envy plagued her. However, they had no idea she was confused as they were, with absolutely no sense of direction, having her life dictated by her parents. She rebelled and took the path presented to her by her peers as they all did, only she had access to destroy her life further with the money.

Wanda understood her and took her under her wings instantly. As she drew an enormous amount of attraction with her expensive clothes and incredible looks, her persona stood out. Wanda admired her for that because she always wanted to acquire those traits for herself. Not to mention, she had access to some very prominent people around the city that became an asset to her later. They had made plans to meet up once they completed the program, being Wanda was only there a week before she arrived. Nevertheless, they were destined to be around each other as they vowed to never part.

They did everything together, sharing their most intimate secrets, and advising one another of their mistakes. They also made plans to go into business together when they returned to society in the following months ahead.

The next day as Doug entered his office, he received the fax from Wanda that read, "Urgent, I need to see you ASAP." Thinking to himself, he wondered what she could possibly want. He knew she wouldn't want to meet about something that was not important. However, it had to wait until later on, as he had a lunch date with Cassandra, that he had no intentions of breaking. And how she managed to send that fax was a mystery to him because he knew she was not allowed outside contact, other than emergencies. He decided to find out what she wanted right away. He contacted the facility to inform them he would be coming today. He then phoned Cassandra and postponed their lunch date, hoping that he could make it up to her at a later date.

Upon arriving at the center, he noticed the same blue Firebird that had followed him from before, a few car lengths behind him. He decided to pull over in order to catch a glimpse of the driver. He noticed they turned off before reaching him, and his curiosity soared as to who this mysterious individual was and what was their motive for watching him.

He waited in the visitation area as Wanda came strolling through the door, looking lavishly appealing. However, her demeanor was totally the opposite, as he soon found out.

"Hi beautiful, you're looking great," he said smoothly.

"Don't give me that, I can't believe you have the nerve to exploit yourself nude on the internet," she said angrily.

"What?" Doug responded dumbfounded to her accusation.

"Are you going to sit there and deny it?" she replied.

"Deny what, baby?" he shot back. Wanda threw the photos she had copied into his lap, and then looked at him, waiting for his response. Doug looked at the photos, totally surprised, wondering how Veronica could betray him without his consent. He explained that he had no idea she was secretly videotaping them and posting them for profit. Somehow Wanda believed him and reasoned that he had to get her out of his life. He promised to do that ASAP. Thrilled that she didn't blow things out of proportion and forgave him, he couldn't wait to confront Veronica about what she had done. After finishing his visit and conversing about their son and how things were going to be, he kissed her before departing. Doug felt furious that he had been exploited in such a manner without his knowledge or consent. Once he reached the townhouse, he encountered Veronica lying on the sofa watching a movie that was homemade.

"So that's how you get your kicks?" he asked her angrily.

"What's wrong with it?" she responded innocently hoping he would calm down, knowing he wasn't supposed to find out until she was long gone.

"That's no excuse. I've been good to you, trusted you and this is how you repay me?" he shouted loud. Sensing his anger, she rose to her feet and approached him, wrapping her arms around him and planting a kiss on his lips. Doug pushed her away in anger to where she stumbled backwards, across the coffee table, bumping her head.

Realizing she might be hurt, he quickly reached down and picked her up, making sure she was alright.

"Doug, I didn't mean to hurt you, I needed money. I've been running from someone and this is how I've been making my living for the past year," she told him honestly.

"Then why didn't you tell me? I would have been receptive of it."

"I didn't know how," she responded sarcastically.

"Well, I can no longer trust you," he informed her. She rubbed her hands on his legs arousing his manhood, while tenderly kissing him and looking into his eyes. She did this knowing his weakness for it. Slowly she eased his dick in her mouth and sucked graciously until he exploded. She continuously drained every drop of juice he had in him, making him become weak, until she made him erect enough to straddle his hardness and ride him to oblivion, enhancing her climax as well. Both were satisfied to the point where the photos were not an issue anymore.

"Veronica you are going to have to move out of here," he told her bluntly.

Shocked that he made the request, she thought she would have to convince him further. "Why?" she responded curiously.

"I think it would be best. Besides, I have a much larger place, where you will be more comfortable," he replied, refusing to tell her the real reason he wanted her out.

"When do you want me to move?" she asked him.

"Tomorrow. I will see things in motion. So you need to get your things packed and ready, the movers will take care of the rest," he said.

"Alright, I'll handle it," she responded, kissing him gently. She teased him until he was aroused again, refusing to let him go before he was fully satisfied, as only she could do. She made sure she got her ass plugged immensely as she raised her ass high in the air, giving him total access. Doug enjoyed fucking her in the ass because she made him feel as though he was magnificent in every aspect. He pounded her hard as she moaned in pleasure, reaching her peak. She exploded from the hard thrust he gave with every stroke, amazed at how she climaxed when he fucked her hard in the ass that way.

Cassandra was enjoying their meal together, talking about the events of her day with her students, as Doug listened carefully wondering how nice and calm she always seemed. "How do you manage to stay so cheerful?" he asked her.

"Actually, I don't, I guess you perceive what you think you see, when in reality it's totally the opposite," she expressed honestly.

"And why is that?" Doug asked her.

"I have my share of problems also. I just try not to let it show, because I do not want others dwelling on them as well," she said softly.

"What problems, if you don't mind me asking?" he responded.

"Well, my husband presents most of them. He's a constant liar and he sleeps around as if it's alright, never concerned about me or even think about being respectable," she informed him with a serious tone.

"Why not consider getting him completely out of your life," he implied.

"That's easier said than done. I've threatened him already with a divorce, that's been to no avail, because he knows I'm not serious," she said

"Then follow through with it, and show him," Doug responded, hoping she would consider it for him.

"I can't," she shot back. "Because I truly love him and I've never been with anyone else other than you. Basically, he's my life and I vowed to spend it with him until death do us part, I cherish those vows. I was hoping he would too eventually," she told him.

"But that's absurd, when someone is totally using you," Doug responded. Suddenly, Cassandra looked up to see Kiana and her husband walk in the door. Capturing their attention, she invited them to her table to eliminate any more conversation about her husband between her and Doug.

"Hey, how yawl doing?" Cassandra asked as they sat down.

"Great, what about yourself sis?" Kiana responded, looking over at Doug smiling. Her husband never said a word, as Doug noticed some tension.

"Can I order something for you?" Doug implied.

"Sure, I'm starving, what's good?" Kiana replied.

"We're enjoying the steaks, would y'all like to have some, or do you prefer the veal?" he asked looking at her husband.

"Whatever!" her husband responded. After ordering and receiving their meal, they engaged in conversation. Doug was considering whether or not he should reveal that Veronica posted their antics on the internet. However, he couldn't stop staring at Kiana sitting in front of him, with a low cut blouse exposing her breasts. Cassandra noticed how he kept staring and directed his attention elsewhere intentionally, distracting everyone. Doug ordered drinks for everyone and collected the bill before they exited and drove their separate ways.

"Doug, why were you staring at my sister?" Cassandra asked him.

"Was I staring?" he responded.

"Yes, constantly. Her husband noticed also," she implied.

"I didn't realize I was doing it at all," he responded.

"I can't help but wonder why?" she replied.

"Do I detect a little bit of insecurity on your behalf?" Doug asked.

"Maybe, but not concerning my sister, cause she would never do anything out of that nature against me," she exclaimed. Suddenly, Doug almost flipped the script, but regained his composure as his cell phone rang.

"Hello," he answered.

"Mr. Walsh, I think you need to come home. Your son has found something that might be of interest to you," The young nanny responded.

"What is it?" Doug responded.

"I think you would want to see this firsthand," she replied sounding serious.

"Alright, I'll be there shortly, Sonya," he informed her before hanging up. After dropping Cassandra over Alicia's house, he headed to the estate. "What's so important?" he asked the nanny.

"My heart dropped when I saw Doug Jr. pulling this out," she said, referring to the contents of the shoe boxes. Doug opened the box to discover over $100,000, and realized the money had to be Wanda's because she was the only one that had access to that room and they were her shoe boxes.

"I never knew this was here, it must belong to Wanda, but why would she hide this amount of money in shoe boxes? That doesn't make sense," he told the young girl as she looked on, shocked that he never knew the money was there. Luckily she could be trusted. "I guess that today is your lucky day Sonya," he told her smiling while admiring her honesty. Not to mention that he liked her, and she was great with Doug, Jr. She kept his mind at ease with the way she bonded so well with him, as he was fond of her also. "I'm going to take you and Doug on a shopping spree tomorrow," he said.

"Really?" she replied happily.

"Dad, can we have whatever we want?" Doug Jr. asked excitedly.

"Sure, whatever you want son," he responded.

"Great! Sonya too?" he shot back.

"Sure, and Sonya now you can buy that car you liked so much and we can ride in that instead of catching the bus or walking," he told her.

"Doug, I don't think your father meant shopping spree like that. It's too expensive," she shot back.

"He said anything, right Dad?" Doug Jr. replied, looking at his father.

"I guess you have me there son, I did say anything. What kind of car were you looking at Sonya?" he asked her smiling.

Shocked and elated she was about to receive a car, she almost forgot what kind it was at the moment. "Are you sure Mr. Walsh?" she asked excited.

"Yes, I'm sure Sonya. What kind of car is it?" he asked again.

"It's brand new, sitting in the showroom window, a Toyota Celica, burgundy and white interior," said Sonya.

"Well, consider it yours, my dear. You earned it," he told her smiling.

Sonya could not believe her ears. "Thank you, thank you so much Mr. Walsh," she responded hugging him tightly, holding on much longer than he expected and arousing him. He knew she was off limits, considering whose daughter she was, and how he was inclined with her mother. However, they looked forward to the next day.

Meanwhile, Cassandra had come home and managed to make it in her room, undetected by Alicia, who had Calvin over for the night. When suddenly she overheard Alicia and Calvin arguing about Calvin getting one of his old girlfriends pregnant, bringing back old memories. She thought her husband was sleeping around on her, which was bringing problems in her marriage. Desperately wanting to dismiss those thoughts, she phoned Kiana.

"Hello," Kiana answered softly.

"Are you in bed?" Cassandra asked her.

"Actually, I'm not sleepy sis, what's up?" she responded.

"Alicia and Calvin are feuding and I need some way to distract myself from it," she told her.

"Feuding about what?" she asked in return.

"I have no idea," Cassandra replied, refusing to reveal her business. "The noise is very distracting, I can't take it," she exclaimed.

"Then come spend the night with me." Kiana suggested.

"That might not be such a bad idea. I'll be right over," she replied. Cassandra quickly packed her things and headed for Kiana's house, which was only five minutes away. She arrived and settled in the extra room where she began finishing her paper peacefully. Kiana came into the room, questioning her about Alicia and Calvin, amongst various other things. Kiana had no interest at the time, until she eventually fell off to sleep right there in the room. Cassandra often wondered about her little sister, knowing she had issues, and continued grading her papers until the phone rang. Kiana, undisturbed by the sound never moved as she was in a deep sleep from the alcohol she drank.

Cassandra answered it. "Hello?" she said.

"Girl, I'm glad you're still up." The voice on the other end stated.

"I wanted to explain something to you before Doug told you and you got the wrong idea," she blurted before Cassandra could tell her she wasn't Kiana. Curious, she played along wanting to hear more now.

"What is it?" she asked, sounding like Kiana.

"Doug discovered that I put our sexual fling on the internet and became furious, but I eventually calmed him down. I wanted to let you know, I never meant to hurt either of you, it's just, I've been making my living off of doing this. I used to be a call girl and wanted out, so I decided to up and leave. However, that wasn't in the cards and I have been running ever since. I hope you understand that I meant no harm. Please forgive me," she said lowly.

Cassandra was shocked and became angry as if she really was Kiana. "How in the hell could you do something so stupid?" Cassandra shot back.

"I'm sorry, please forgive me." The voice responded.

"I'm not Kiana, I'm her sister, Cassandra, you dumb bitch. It's a good thing I don't know who you are cause you wouldn't like me very much," she shouted before hanging up on her.

Cassandra was highly upset as she stared at her sister sleeping. She wondered why she would do something so stupid, let alone against her. She then focused all her anger on Doug. Now she knew why he kept staring at Kiana earlier that night. She couldn't believe he had been unfaithful to her, and to think it was her sister was unimaginable.

Cassandra debated on whether she should wake Kiana and ask her, but decided that it wasn't a good time because she wasn't stable enough to discuss this reasonably. Therefore, she opted to wait, and confront her and Doug at the most appropriate time together. She then woke Kiana to go to bed. Constantly tossing and turning as she thought about the devastating news she had just heard. She wanted to confront the woman responsible also. In time she would get to the bottom of it.

The next day, Doug made arrangements for the car and had it sent to the estate, gift wrapped for Sonya, who was elated once she arrived and saw it in the garage. They headed for the mall; she drove as if the car was made for her, smiling from ear to ear. Doug noticed how thrilled she was to have her own vehicle. However, he wondered what her mother would say about him purchasing her the car. Nevertheless, he was happy to do it for her because she was close to his son and he felt she really deserved it. They entered the mall and begun purchasing an enormous amount of clothing and accessories, having fun as though they were a family.

"Let's get something to eat, I'm hungry," Doug Jr. said.

"That's a good idea, what you want to eat?" His father asked him.

"Hot dogs!" He shouted in excitement. Sonya laughed, knowing he was taking advantage of his father's kindness as he often did at any given moment. However, Doug honored his request, since he rarely found time to do anything with him on a regular basis. As they sat eating, he watched closely as Doug Jr. ate furiously. The thought of his son happy, filled him with a sense of joy that made him proud to be his father.

"Sonya, thank you, you can't imagine how much you've helped me in his mother's absence," Doug expressed to her openly.

"Thank you Mr. Walsh. I like him, we're friends. It's the least I could do and you've helped me also in more ways than you know. If there is anything that you need, I mean anything, don't hesitate to ask, because there is no limit to what I will do for you. Between us, no limit," she told him with a serious look in her eyes, throwing a hint.

Doug did take a second look as he realized exactly what she meant. Although she was a very attractive teenager, he had no intentions of getting sexually involved with her, even though it was enticing. "I'll remember that if I ever happen to require those services from you one day," he shot back, acknowledging her hint.

"Good, I'll be sure to make myself available," she informed him.

After spending about five hours in the mall shopping, they were all tired and drained when they returned home. They sat around talking while eating ice cream. Doug Jr. went upstairs and took a nap. Eventually Doug and Sonya fell asleep on the sofa.

Cassandra woke late on Saturday morning and headed to the shower. Upon reaching Kiana's bedroom, she heard moaning sounds, and continued to the bathroom. After showering and putting on her clothes, she headed for the kitchen. There she encountered Kiana and her coworker, Tenita drinking coffee.

"Good morning sis, did you sleep well?" Kiana asked.

"As well as to be expected, considering the circumstances," she shot back.

"Oh, this is my friend Tenita, we work together," Kiana exclaimed.

"Hello," Tenita responded.

"Hi, glad to meet you," Cassandra expressed politely. "Where is your husband, Kiana?" Cassandra asked curiously.

"He left early this morning. He fishes on Saturday," she responded.

"Oh," Cassandra replied, knowing it was her and Tenita in the room together. She had heard her sister liked girls. But this was the first time she ever encountered it for herself. However, she had to devise a plan to get them and Doug together, so that she could confront them about their sexual escapade. She was still highly upset that they could betray her, knowing she cared deeply for them both and would never do anything out of character to hurt either of them in any way. "So do you have any plans for today?" Cassandra asked her sister as she was tense looking at her friend.

"Actually, we were going to just hang around the house today, and relieve some stress," She responded in return.

"Would y'all like to accompany me to lunch with Doug?" Cassandra asked, hoping they would agree.

"We'd only be in the way. I'm sure you would prefer being alone with your man, wouldn't you sis?" Kiana responded.

"It's no big deal, I'll enjoy your company," Cassandra explained softly, hoping to entice her to come.

"Maybe some other time. We're going to chill around here and wait for our husbands to come back. We're going to have a fish fry this evening, maybe you could bring Doug over here," Kiana suggested.

"That's perfect," she responded, knowing this would be the appropriate place to bring it all out in the open and reveal everything, including her fling with Tenita in front of their husbands.

"We're expecting them back around five this evening," Kiana informed her. "I'm calling Alicia and Calvin too, hopefully they are still not feuding, so we can all get together tonight," Kiana expressed happily.

"That's a good idea," Cassandra exclaimed, knowing she wouldn't be smiling once she revealed her little secret in front of everyone. She had to be taught a lesson about screwing around with men her sister was involved with and learn some respect the hard way.

Doug and Sonya laid sleeping when the phone rang, awakening Sonya as Doug continued to sleep.

"Hello?" Sonya answered in a low tone.

"Who's speaking?" Cassandra asked, curious as to who was answering the phone.

"I'm Sonya, Doug Jr. nanny," she responded in return wondering who was asking questions, "Who's calling?" she replied curiously.

"This is Cassandra. I'm a friend of Doug, is he there?" she asked.

"He's sleeping right now, can I take a message?" she shot back.

"Will you tell him I said to meet me at my sister Kiana's house at six o'clock tonight. It's very important, please don't forget," she told her.

"Sure, I'll tell him when he wakes up," Sonya responded.

"Thank you," She said before hanging up.

Sonya placed the receiver down and glanced over at Doug lying on the sofa. She was upset by the phone call, thinking the woman wasn't suitable for a man of his caliber. As thoughts ran through her mind, she walked over to the sofa and sat beside the sleeping Doug . After touching him softly, noticing he didn't respond, she unzipped his zipper and stuck her hand inside his pants, feeling his dick. Doug didn't respond, she then pulled his dick out and began to suck it slowly; going up and down the shaft as if it was a lollipop, graciously until it was rock hard.

Doug eased his eyes open as he felt her tender hot lips on the head of his dick. Shocked at the sight of what was happening, he couldn't stop her as he enjoyed it so much. Sonya noticed he wasn't about to resist and gradually picked up the pace as she began sucking up and down the shaft of his manhood, looking into his eyes and capturing his facial expression as she aroused him with an intense pleasure.

"Oh, I'm almost there, don't stop," he told her in a low tone. At that moment, he exploded in her mouth and she gracefully swallowed every drop of juice he squirted, continuously sucking until he became erect again. Lying in a trance, Doug couldn't move. Sonya rose and quickly removed her clothes. She straddled him and pushed his hard dick up in her slowly. She began riding as though she had to have him deep inside her, moaning loud. Doug couldn't believe the sight on top of him, as she revealed her luscious breast bouncing up and down, with her firm round ass, pounding into his pelvis with each thrust she presented. Overwhelmed, he then stopped her and placed her on the sofa. He pushed her legs up and pounded hard thrusts into her as she screamed loudly, enjoying the massive hardness penetrating her immensely until she climaxed; grabbing his arms, squeezing him tightly before he released his load into her. He collapsed on top of her breathing hard. "That was nice Mr. Walsh," Sonya told him softly.

"Sonya, no one can find out about this," he explained.

"It might be a little too late for that," Sonya told him.

"What do you mean?" he asked concerned. "Turn around and look," she said as Doug Jr. looked on.

Doug turned around as Doug Jr. took off back upstairs laughing. At least he wasn't upset by what he saw, Doug thought to himself. Hopefully, he wouldn't bring this up and reveal what he saw to anyone, as Sonya hadn't yet turned 18 for another two weeks.

"I don't think we have anything to worry about, I'll talk to him and keep him quiet, he listens to me." Sonya told him, to assure his confidence in them both.

"Alright, but keep me informed just in case," he told her.

"I will Mr. Walsh. Besides, I look forward to this again, and I'm not about to let him ruin it for us," she expressed.

"I must admit you are feisty," he told her.

"Really?" she shot back.

"I'm sure you've heard that before," he told her smiling.

"Actually, you're the first," she exclaimed. "No, I mean the first man I've ever been with, that's why I enforced it. I was curious to find out," she told him.

"What you're a virgin?" he shouted at her. "I was but not anymore, thanks to you Mr. Walsh. My cherry belongs to you now," she said, laughing out loud.

"I should've used protection," he said.

"That's no problem, the chance of me being pregnant is 100 in 1. Oh, by the way, your friend Cassandra called and told me to tell you to meet her by six o'clock at her sister Kiana's house."

"Then I guess I had better get showered and ready to go," he told her.

CHAPTER 14

Rita was lost in thought in the office of her newly acquired beauty salon. While watching the cars go by during lunch hour traffic, she noticed Michelle pulling into the parking lot. She wondered what she could possibly want since they weren't in the least bit fond of each other. And how did she know about the salon?

"Hello Rita, I'm glad I caught you here, I need to talk to you concerning Doug Walsh. I'm sure you're aware of him firing me. Well, we need to come up with a plan to acquire what's ours and teach that bastard a lesson," she expressed angrily.

"Hold up Missy. First of all, what do you mean we? And secondly, he doesn't have anything that belongs to us, so where do you get off coming over here with that bullshit?" Rita shot back.

"Don't tell me, he got you hooked too?" Michelle asked in anger.

"Doug has helped me in many ways. Even after I explained to him about our plot, he still trusted and forgave me, and there's no way I'm about to cross him again under any circumstances. Besides, I'm pregnant with his child, so you're fishing in the wrong pond. Still waters run deep around here now." Rita expressed frankly.

"You're what? I can't believe you would stoop that low. I mean, you're married to my cousin," she shot back.

"Who we coincidentally haven't heard from after he received the money. Wake the hell up. Can't you see he hauled ass and left us holding the bag? What part don't you understand, or are you stupid?" Rita shouted angrily.

"Ain't that the kettle calling the pot black. You don't even have a clue, he doesn't give a damn about you. He has Wanda as his first interest, not to mention the other women out there. Hell, he was fucking me two or three times a week. So don't think you're the love of his life. You're just another piece of ass." Michelle told her as she looked intensely in her face.

"Regardless of what you say or think, I'm not about to help you. So you need to leave my shop, which he purchased for me, in case you didn't know, Ms. Thang," Rita said sarcastically.

"Oh, I see. He's already manipulated you too, because you can't see the forest for the trees." Michelle expressed harshly.

"That's alright, as long as I realize they're woods," she shot back.

"So you don't mind competing with other women?" Michelle implied.

"As long as he acknowledges and takes care of me, I have no problem with what he had before me," she told her in a serious tone.

"I thought you were smarter than that, but I see you're accustomed to sloppy seconds as long as you get something." Michelle expressed sharply.

"That's better than using someone for selfish gains," Rita shot back.

"I take it you forgot we were all in this together? You didn't have any problem with selfish gains then, did you?" she said angrily.

"Well, I've had a change of heart and I'm not thinking of doing anything that will jeopardize our relationship now. Besides, I'm financially secure to live comfortable," she told her.

"And how long do you think that's going to last?" Michelle came back.

"No matter how long it lasts, you're wasting your time here, because I have no intentions of helping you, so leave my shop now!"

"Sure thing, I'll leave but you're going to wish you would've listened in the end, because I will come out on top." Michelle told her angrily.

"I'd like to know how you're going to accomplish that," she shot back.

"Because I've got something you don't." Michelle told her.

"And what's that?" Rita asked in return.

"Everything isn't for everybody, however in time you'll find out." Michelle stated as she headed for the door, leaving Rita in suspense, wondering what she was implying.

Meanwhile, Kiana and Tenita had cleaned the large bucket of fish and prepared everything to deep fry. Kiana had invited Alicia and Calvin, along with Veronica, who had showed up capturing everyone's attention with her outlandish outfit which revealed half her ass. This astonished Cassandra, who had no idea she was the one that called to reveal the threesome over the phone last night. They soon became acquainted right away.

Everyone was there listening to music, drinking and having a good time, as they waited for the fish to start frying. However, Cassandra couldn't wait for Doug to arrive as she now became furious thinking about what happened between him and her sister, which she acted as if it never occurred. Watching her and Tenita only made matters worse because she was also having an affair as her husband sat around innocently. She wondered how he was going to respond once he found out what was going on around him and right in front of his face. Doug arrived as Cassandra met him at the door. They mingled as everyone seemed to be having a good time. She hadn't decided how or when she would bring up the incident; however, she was biding her time for the right moment.

The kids were playing in one area as the grownups listened to the music blaring loudly. Kiana and her husband were frying the fish, as Calvin strolled over to give them a hand. Veronica noticed Doug with Cassandra and began to feel out of place. So she lowered her head before he looked her way.

"Why didn't you let me know what was going on here?" Doug asked, as he noticed his surroundings.

"Does it really matter?" Cassandra responded in return.

"Under the circumstances, I guess not as long as we're together, but I would've preferred to know beforehand," he replied.

"Loosen up we're here to have a good time," she expressed softly.

However, Doug thought otherwise, since Veronica kept staring his way, looking as though she was uptight about something. At that moment, Calvin called out to Doug, waving him over to the grill, as Kiana looked up, catching his eye. As he approached, Cassandra kept a close eye on them both.

"What's up man? I haven't seen you in a while, what's been going on?" he asked him.

"Not much, just taking it one day at a time," Doug responded.

"I need to talk some business with you later," Calvin told him.

"Alright, I'll be around," Doug responded.

"I hope you like fish, Doug?" Kiana said with a smile.

"Sure" He responded as the others looked on.

"Of course, we do have other selections in case you don't" Her husband responded quickly. Suddenly Alicia came over, grabbing Calvin by the arm.

"That's what I like about a man," she complimented.

"And what's that?" Calvin asked.

"He's not choosy, easy to please," she replied, smiling, while Doug listened in.

"So, you think I am?" Calvin shot back.

"Most of the time," she responded. Calvin jerked his arm away and walked off, as though he was upset by her comment.

"Men are so touchy." Kiana responded, looking at Alicia as she watched Calvin.

"That's not true; women get upset more than men, mostly about nothing." Her husband responded.

"How did you arrive at that conclusion? You're really jealous," Kiana said laughing.

"Because women are more emotional than men," he replied.

"That's because we love more in-depth.' Alicia added.

"And men mostly think of themselves in that aspect, especially during sex.' Kiana stated firmly.

"That's a double standard." Cassandra shouted.

"Sis, I know you're taking their side." Kiana shot back.

"It's not about taking sides; it's a state of being we all possess. However, some women who are the sum of all these things actually have no knowledge of them and don't think before acting out, thereby creating problems for themselves and other as well." Cassandra stated, looking serious.

"But that doesn't give them a reason not to care." Kiana responded.

"And it does justify you not giving a damn either." Cassandra replied.

"I do care when I feel it's appropriate and deserved," she said.

"By your standards, which ain't necessarily correct, because if you're not benefiting, it's not right is it?" Cassandra stated sharply. Everyone became quiet as Kiana realized her sister had a point she couldn't deny, she had to find a way out.

"I see no reason, if it's not beneficial to me," she responded.

"That's my point, because you don't care whether it hurts

someone else in the process. You only care about yourself." Cassandra shouted loudly.

"That's their problem. I can't spend time thinking about everybody and their feelings. That's not my responsibility," she stated frankly.

"That's where you're wrong, you've been running for years," Suddenly Alicia broke in.

"Cassandra, this has gone too far, change the subject."

"No, this needs to be said right now. You've been running round for years hurting people and it never seems to bother you. Well, maybe you should have feelings for others before you do it, because you're no better than anyone else," Cassandra expressed with emotion.

"Well, that's not my fault. I'm not here to live up to someone else's expectations, only my own," Kiana screamed.

"I agree. What you do is your business, but when it affects your husband, your friends and your family, including me, you've got a problem, cause I'm not having it by any means," Cassandra shot back angrily.

"Well, what I do doesn't affect you." Kiana responded back.

"That's where you're wrong. I love you and I trusted you, but now all that's in the past, because you're no good and regardless of whether you're my sister or not, that's no excuse." Now they all were silent, listening as Cassandra talked. "Right is right and wrong isn't in the cards concerning this. I can't believe you stooped this low."

"What the hell are you talking about?" Kiana shouted.

"The way you have been spreading yourself thin with any and everybody. Don't question my integrity, you're not stupid. So why are you playing dumb?" Cassandra yelled.

"Why are you in my business?" Kiana shouted angrily.

"Because it concerns me," She shot back loudly.

"Nothing I do concerns you." Kiana replied.

"Then explain these." Cassandra then realized Veronica was the one who called, the moment she pulled out the pictures, she had retrieved from the computer before she threw them on the table in front of her. Kiana was speechless, this was the first time she had seen or even heard about what was before her. She looked over at Doug and Veronica, hoping they would help explain, neither said a word. Her husband and everyone else looked on, surprised as anger built within them both. Suddenly her husband burst.

"What the hell, you out your damn mind?" he shouted.

"I had no idea I was being photographed. Veronica, did you know about this?" she asked, desperate for an answer.

"I can explain" She said softly. "Don't act surprised, you been doing it all along, and your friend over there acting innocent isn't any better. Yes! I'm speaking of you, how long you been messing round on your husband? I heard you and Kiana this morning as I got up to take a shower." Cassandra blurted, tired of the fact people around her were cheating on one another, she had been through enough with her husband.

"What, you too?" Tenita's husband shouted.

"We'll talk about it at home," she told him.

"No, we can talk about it right now. I kinda figured you were messing around, but I had no idea it was with a woman."

Tempers were flying and everyone was on edge now. Kiana walked over to Veronica and asked her to explain. Cassandra sensed her anger setting in and started telling the whole story for her. The minute she finished, Kiana raised her hand and slapped Veronica as hard as she could, knocking her to the ground. Doug pulled her away before she could continue her attack, as Cassandra helped her up. Her husband confronted Doug as to how he could act as though he had no part in it. Calvin stepped in and stopped any ruckus before they got started, while Cassandra finished telling the story.

"There's no need of you being mad, you betrayed me as she betrayed you, so which one of ya'll should carry the burden?" she said looking at them both.

"How do you think I felt when I heard this last night? I couldn't believe my ears, but I could believe my eyes, once I saw the pictures," Cassandra stated.

"That's still no excuse," Tenita's husband shouted as he stormed out. She looked at Cassandra furious and ran after him.

"I feel the same way. You don't have any respect for me, there isn't any excuse." Kiana stated, going in the house and closing the door.

"I hope you're happy now, sis. You managed to piss everyone off, running your mouth," Kiana shouted loud.

"But I spoke the truth, I have no remorse," she shouted back.

Kiana headed into the house to explain to her husband. Doug

gave Veronica some ice wrapped in a rag as her face was swollen and red, while Cassandra looked on. Calvin asked Alicia if she was ready to go, as Kiana returned and apologized to Veronica before she left. However, they were all mad at each other and furious with Cassandra for spilling the beans.

"There's nothing I can say, it just happened. I'm sorry, hopefully you can forgive me." Doug told Cassandra.

"Why did it have to be my sister?" she asked him.

"It just happened," he stated

"I've been through enough with my husband, now I'm subjected to more. I can't live like this, it's hard for me to put trust in anyone anymore," she expressed bluntly. "I thought what we had was special, but it's obvious you didn't seem to think so, by screwing my sister and another woman simultaneously," she told him in tears.

"I said I'm sorry." Doug told her.

"Well, that's not going to cut it. I can't accept that. I trusted and loved you, which meant nothing to you, cause you really hurt me and I have hurt my family. Therefore, I feel it's best we don't see one another anymore, at least for a while. Maybe things will change, however, I don't think they will ever be the same," she cried.

"But we can work this out, I love you," he shouted.

"I see no need pursuing it any further right now," she said, as she wiped tears from her eyes and walked away.

Doug was devastated as he stood there looking up, wishing he hadn't made that fatal mistake. He walked to the side of the house and watched Cassandra as she pulled away. Many thoughts ran through his mind as he drove home. What a mess he had made of it all. Somehow, he had to find a way to fix it, as part of him was lost. Upon opening the door, he was happily greeted by his son. At least someone still loved him, he thought to himself. After hugging him, he decided to go to bed for the night.

Meanwhile, Kiana and her husband discussed the incident.

"I can't believe you did this to me! That's three affairs in one. You have absolutely no respect for me!" He told her.

"It's not like that, I love you. You knew about me liking women before we were married, and what do you want me to do?" Kiana asked.

"You not only had an affair with two women, a man was involved also. That's totally out of character. It reveals your infidelity and disrespect for me. I'm your husband, we both took those vows together. Didn't they mean anything to you?" he shouted in anger, knowing he was guilty also.

"It's done, I can't change it. I'm sorry, it won't happen again. What more can I do?" As she moved closer, caressing him, she aroused his desire. He grabbed her and roughly tore off her blouse, exposing her breast. She tore his shirt and they stripped each other. Upon pushing her onto the bed, he penetrated her and cupped her ass with both hands as she lifted her legs, giving him access. He pounded hard strokes, deep up in her as he pulled her to him intensely. Kiana screamed passionately as he drilled her with deep hard thrusts, pushing her to climax immediately. They continued through the night, satisfying one another.

Calvin and Alicia arrived home only to find Cassandra packing her things, attempting to leave.

"What are you doing?" Alicia asked concerned.

"I'm leaving, I don't want to be a burden, where I'm not wanted, after what happened tonight," She told her.

"Whatever gave you that idea? You're always welcome here. You only told the truth and they have to respect that, even if you stepped on their toes doing it. I don't fault you and I'm not holding any grudges, so you stay here as long as you want... Besides, you don't want to move back with your husband anyway." Alicia told her.

"Are you sure?" Cassandra replied, making sure she was welcomed.

"Of course...why wouldn't I be sis?" she responded.

Tenita had another problem; she was trying to convince her husband not to leave, as he started packing his bags. He was dead set on leaving and there was nothing she could say to persuade him otherwise. He left the same night.

Veronica had a tremendous headache when she got home, so she took some medication and went to bed. She regretted ever meeting any of them and pondered whether she should leave and move on somewhere else. Only time would tell her fate, as she debated in her mind what was her best option. However, she decided, once she had time, to discuss the situation with Doug.

The next day, she made phone calls home, trying to find out if it would be safe for her to return. However, she still had her doubts about being in the city, because it only presented more problems for her. But she didn't want to continue living this way.

That Monday at work, Tenita informed Kiana that her husband had left her that night, and she didn't think he would return. Kiana told her that she went through similar drama. However, her husband wasn't really concerned about her being involved with women, but was more upset about her being involved with Doug, which was his main objective.

"As if he hasn't messed around on you. Ain't that a bitch. Men are dogs," she expressed angrily, looking at Kiana.

"I can't complain. He's been faithful to me." Kiana said openly.

"Yeah, right!" Tenita responded nonchalantly.

"You don't know my husband." Kiana said snobbishly.

"And you don't either, if you believe that," she shot back.

"What you mean by that?" Kiana asked harshly.

"Let's test him and see." Tenita suggested. "Set him up and see how faithful he is, unless you're scared. Shit, I don't think he's faithful at all," she said knowing he wasn't.

"And how do you propose to do it?" she asked her.

"I'll lure him while you're in my house, then you can see for yourself," she explained.

"Alright!" She agreed.

Later that evening, Kiana called home and informed her husband she would be working late. Meanwhile, Tenita called him and enticed him to come over, while Kiana sat in the other room listening. Before he arrived, Tenita put on a blue teddy, revealing her ass cheeks and luscious breast. Kiana was aroused when she saw her in it.

Her husband came in and wasted no time caressing her breast, rubbing all over her pretty brown round ass. The minute they engaged, Kiana walked to the door of the bedroom. But instead of getting mad, she was more enticed to join them. At least now she no longer had to hide or feel guilty anymore.

"Are you enjoying yourself?" she asked as her husband was deep in Tenita from behind. Shocked, he stopped and looked around only to see his wife standing there stark naked, and looking good.

"Oh, you set me up, huh?" he said smiling.

"Don't worry; the more the merrier. I ain't mad at you," she said as she lay beside them on the bed. They all continued as if they were meant to be together, satisfying one another's desire beyond any doubt.

~ ~ ~ ~

Later that day, Doug entered the therapist's office, lonely and depressed, as he settled in for his session, things were rather bleak, Dr. Williams noticed right away from his anxieties.

"Seems you're tense about something...what is it?" she asked him.

"Nothing ...just stressed out with business affairs," he informed her.

"Sometimes you have to let go...and relax without thinking so much about what's not going right...because regardless of who you are or what it's concerning...things don't always go as you plan them...or the way you want...so why worry about something you can't control," she said with a smile.

"That's interesting because I have been thinking a lot about you lately...and it's gotten to the point where I can't control it now," he shot back.

"That's infatuation, because you're not interested in me," she told him.

"And what makes you so sure of that?" Doug asked.

"Because you haven't made any notion towards me," she informed him.

"I'm doing it now and you're neglecting it," he said smiling.

"Really? Is that what you feel?" she asked him.

"Yes, because I want to get to know you better," he implied smoothly.

"In what way Mr. Walsh?" she responded.

"Intimately!" Doug stated sharply.

Humored by his honesty, she hesitated as he caught her completely off-guard. "How do you plan on accomplishing this task? You know absolutely nothing about me," she responded in return.

"That's what I'm attempting to find out. So, are you willing to give me that chance?" he asked her seriously.

"I guess I could, considering you're an interesting prospect and you're persistent. Not to mention various other things that do arouse my curiosity," she stated loosely.

"My session is over. Now you can explore the real me and come to the proper conclusion of what you think my problem really is," he said with a wink.

"I guess now is a good time, but I must go home first. My pets have to be fed," she told him.

"No problem. I'm curious to see how you're living since I've never encountered the lifestyle of a doctor before," he said.

As they finished up, Dr. Williams locked up and they headed towards her house. Doug followed her into a classy, well-manicured neighborhood adorned with fancy houses, spaced graciously apart from one another. When she pulled in the driveway of her mansion, he was impressed by the look of things. He had no idea she lived so well, he couldn't wait to see the interior.

Once inside, he was amazed at its lovely beauty, she had good taste. Suddenly a white poodle startled him, rubbing against his leg, as she called out saying his bark was worse than his bite. Doug liked dogs but not in his house. He noticed she had an exotic bird and talked to it. Although its vocabulary wasn't very long, it was rather interesting all the more. He wondered how much of a problem he was, because he thought it would be nice to acquire one himself.

"Would you like a drink, Mr. Walsh?" she asked him as she fed the bird.

"Sure, that would be nice," he responded, watching her. She rang a little bell and a middle aged lady appeared. Doug was shocked as he noticed she had a maid, no wonder the place was immaculately clean.

"Will you bring the drinks to the den?" she informed the maid.

She led Doug down the long hallway before turning into a luscious den, filled with paintings and fine elegant furniture. The place had a calmness he never experienced before, it was unlike his estate. Although his was fancier, hers was more comfortable with a homely feel to it. Doug admired it as much as his own; however, he wanted to see more before he left. "I'll return in a few minutes... make yourself at home," she told him, as she headed upstairs.

The maid returned with the drinks on a tray, and a full bottle of Hennessy. Doug drank his down in one gulp. She opened the bottle to offer him another one, when suddenly he noticed Dr. Williams entering with a pair of white shorts and a tank top on revealing her body. Something he had longed to see, since he started taking sessions with her.

"Dr. Williams, if you no longer need my services...I'm going home." the maid informed her.

"Thank you Mrs. Tyson…I'll see you tomorrow," she said

"Alright…have a nice night," the lady stated as she left.

Dr. Williams sat beside Doug on the sofa, placing one leg under her ass, revealing her inner thighs as she reached for her drink, downing it quickly, and refilling both their glasses.

"So Mr. Walsh, I understand you're not just interested in me…what's your motive?" she asked him. "I really don't have one…other than my desire for you…because I'm already financially stable…money isn't what I'm after…so what makes you think I have one?" he shot back.

"That's funny. My husband said the same thing, but it didn't keep him here that long, so he couldn't have been interested," she said smiling. Doug cut through the chase as he noticed she was rather tipsy now, he then moved in closer.

"I assure you that's it's not the case with me," he stated before planting a wet kiss on her lips. Suddenly she opened up and prolonged any further, wrapping her arms around him. He slipped his hand under her already revealing tank top, exposing her nipples and squeezing them hard. She gasped as her hands went wild, rubbing him all over. Doug then went lower, popping the button on her shorts, sliding them off and exposing the bushy hair around her pussy. He wasted no time getting undressed and entering her. He noticed her tightness and was sure she wasn't active sexually, as she moaned loudly from each stroke. Gradually he let her adjust before he began to enhance his thrust enormously. She climaxed, squeezing him tightly, moaning in passion. Doug was overwhelmed that she was enjoying it as much as he was before easing out, lying beside her. She then suggested they go upstairs to the bedroom. Here they engaged in heavy, hard sex as Doug really pounded her hard, exploding rapidly before collapsing.

"That was long overdue," she said softly.

"I'm glad you enjoyed it," he shot back.

"Yeah, more than you know," she said excitedly.

"Did your daughter tell you about the present I bought her?" he asked.

"Actually, I haven't talked to her in a couple of days. She tries to say she needs her space. I don't agree with her .I try and let her make her own decisions to a certain extent," she told him. "By the way…what did you give her?" she asked curiously.

"A new car," he stated.

"What? Not the one in the showroom?" she asked.

"That's the one," he said. "That little devil, she fell out with me cause I wouldn't buy that car for her. Now she's convinced you to get it. Wait until I see her," she told him.

"What's the problem?" Doug responded.

"My intention was for her to complete college first...then she could purchase something much better. However, it's alright since you were so generous. I'm not complaining," she said.

"I only did it cause my son and her found a large sum of money in the house that belonged to my mother. And I stuck my foot in my mouth saying I was going to take them on a shopping spree, not realizing I didn't put stipulations on it." Doug explained.

"And she took advantage of it?" she asked in return.

"Actually, it was my son who took advantage of it, stating what she wanted and I was forced to concur." Doug told her.

"Kids will be kids, won't they?" she informed him.

CHAPTER 15

On Sunday, Yvonne was sitting around the house relaxing and watching cartoons with her son, spending quality time alone as the phone rang.

"Hello?" she answered.

"How're you doing?" The voice on the other end said as she accepted the automated call.

"Not bad, how about you?" she asked waiting for a response.

"Oh, I'm maintaining, thinking of you," Marquis said smoothly.

"Well…that's nice to know. I'm really flattered that you're so keyed in on me," she said softly.

"So what's good?" he asked curiously.

"I'm just spending time with my son," she exclaimed.

"That's a good gesture cause these are the years where you prime him for life," he said sincerely.

"As long as I can keep him focused on what's important considering he listens and don't go astray," she told him.

"I can relate with that! Ha! I'm a prime example," he said.

"Yeah, but things change. It's inevitable and the most constant thing in life, regardless of whether you want it to or not," she expressed.

"I agree and I thank you for holding me down. Not every woman understands the significance of what it means to have a woman there for you…which is rare in most cases. And that's when they need something or someone to look forward to, although I had no idea you were so keen. You really inspired me in ways that made my life take on a new mission," he said seriously.

"After all, I've experienced, this is challenging. But my instincts tell me it's right and even though it's awkward, it still feels right. And I'll continue to do whatever's in my power to accomplish our task together because I've committed myself to a certain extent and I'll follow through," she said.

"That's what excites me about you; the way you keep your word and stay focused on what you set your mind to. That's a valuable attribute that's hard to find in most people these days," he told her.

"However, there's so much more I want to do, but I'm not able to right now. Hopefully I'll find a way to do them later," she told him.

"I understand, but you're doing great. As long as we keep our communications open and stay on point, it will only get better. However, I realize you're busy with far more important things to do and you can't visit on a regular basis. I can accept the fact that you'll come when you can, but even if it's only once a month, I'm grateful for that cause I know you're real. And that's what matters the most to me," he expressed with concern.

"I will come when time permits, but until then hope that you remain patient And know in your heart that I have you in my best interest. Cause you're important to me," she said.

"I respect that and I'm looking forward to expanding our friendship further as time goes by. I'm hoping to get out as soon as the courts rule on my Certiorari Motion...," he expressed honestly.

"Hopefully things will work out for you in time and I'm sure we'll be able to create what we want together," she said softly.

Rita was determined to get back at Michelle. However, she had no idea that her plans was for everyone else, that she felt sure about. Nevertheless, she wasn't about to let her do anything to hurt Doug because she had all intention of being with him in the end. After contacting Doug, she had thought about how she was going to tell him that she was carrying his baby. She wondered how he would respond when he found out or what he was going to do. She waited patiently for his arrival.

Sonya and Doug Jr. were preparing for a day of fun as they got ready to explore the scenes they had planned to drive upon. Sonya had promised to take him on a day of cruising around in her new car.

"Little Doug, are you finished in there? I need to take a shower before we head out," she hollered loudly as Doug Jr. exited in response.

"Sure, it's all yours now," he said as he came out. Sonya got her things and rushed in to shower, knowing that time was of the essence for what she had planned today. Upon finishing her shower, she discovered she had forgotten her skin lotion in a rush to get ready. "Little Doug, will you get my skin lotion off the bed?" she hollered.

"Okay!" He responded.

Unaware that Sonya had exited the shower, he plunged into the bedroom to find her standing naked. Shocked at the sight of her, he froze, excitedly looking at her body. Something he had never experienced before. Sonya noticed how he stood there in a daze, holding her lotion. She took it out of his hand, never attempting to cover up. Being that he was only eight years old, she felt no harm in letting him view her naked. However, Doug Jr.'s mind was racing with thoughts after seeing her with his father and now first hand for himself. He eased out of the bathroom and glanced around, watching in amazement as she rubbed the lotion all over her body. Little did Sonya know she was creating a monster because Doug Jr. was curiously thinking of what it would be like with her. He was already fond of her and loved having her around, which only increased as he saw her now in another way.

Doug made it to Rita's by midday and entered into the most exotic smelling fragrance he had ever encountered. She had the place looking immaculate all over and fixed lunch for them as they sat watching Soul Train. Rita was sitting there in her house robe next to Doug who was chewing as if he hadn't eaten in days. Suddenly she let her robe fall open while looking in his direction. Doug noticed the minute it parted and kept watching Soul Train as if she didn't exist.

Knowing he had spent an incredible amount of energy all night long on Dr. Williams, he wasn't inspired to do anyone at that particular time. He knew Rita wasn't about to let him leave before he did, though. She then motioned for the remote and clicked off the T.V. Doug knew exactly what that meant, since he hadn't seen her in a week, which was far too long by her standards. She threw her leg across his lap, exposing her inner thighs, delightfully teasing him while rubbing his chest,

"I'll guess you know why I called you?" she whispered softly.

"I think I do baby," Doug shot back.

"I hope you're not going to disappoint me?" she asked.

"Do I ever?" he responded.

"That's what I wanted to hear," she said softly.

Doug ran his hand up her leg and pulled her panties off, throwing them to the floor. He gently kissed her while softly squeezing her breast as she gratefully moaned in pleasure. She eased his pants loose and grabbed his dick, going up and down the length of it. Feeling the warmth of his hardness excited her as she quickly went down and put her warm lips around his head. Doug knew he had to perform as she graciously sucked hard bringing him to a full erection in seconds. He hoped she would stop so he could get this over with. She vigorously kept a tight suction until he exploded in her mouth.

Ignoring his limpness, she kept her pace as she swallowed every drop, bringing him erect again. She then laid back on the sofa and threw one leg over the back, exposing all of her pussy in his face. Doug mounted her, pulling her other leg up high and pushed her hard until he reached her pelvis as she screamed loud upon his every thrust. He pounded into her constantly, moaning with pleasure as she consistently pushed up, meeting every thrust, enhancing their pleasure until they both climaxed together. They were both exhausted from this long overdue experience.

"That was so nice. I needed that so much," she told him.

"I'm glad to be of service," he shot back.

While still unwrapped in his arms, she kissed him gently and rubbed his head until she felt him looking at her. "Doug, I've got to tell you something that I hope you will be happy to hear," she said slowly.

"What is it?" he responded.

"I'm pregnant!" She blurted out quickly.

"What?" he shouted.

"I'm sure you heard me. I would like to think that would have excited you not upset you," she said concerned.

"Shocked? Yeah, that I am. Upset? No. Excited somewhat? In more ways than you can imagine," he shot back.

"What's that supposed to mean?" she asked.

"Nothing we can't handle," he claimed.

"So, what's next?" she asked him.

"We'll prepare for what's expected as usual," he said.

"Does that mean that you're okay with it and you're happy?" she asked.

"It sure does," he told her, totally thinking the opposite.

Wanda and Rhonda sat up through the night talking as Wanda waited for the morning of her release, which came early by surprise.

They made plans to get together once they were released and got back into society. Rhonda was mystified at one point and happy all in one. Showing mixed emotions was normal to her since that's how she felt all her life. Her family had instilled it in her once they decided to mold her life the way they wanted her. She never had the chance to think and choose anything on her own without their input.

But now that she's met Wanda and completed the program, it seemed as though she's been revitalized to think on her own. And now she was about to experience it in ways she never had before.

She had become overwhelmed with Wanda as a friend since they met cause she gave her hope and a new sense of direction to see things for what they really were. This was something she hadn't ever had to do herself for fear of her family's disapproval. She felt she had to please them and live up to their standards, neglecting what she really felt and wanted for herself. Eventually, it took its toll and drove her to doing drugs just to fit in with regular kids her age. Wanda helped her to understand these things and so, she started caring for herself with a sense of belonging she understood.

The next morning, during the time Wanda was signing out, she said to Rhonda, "Take care. I'm really going to miss you girl. And don't forget to contact me if you want. I'll come get you," Wanda exclaimed.

"Don't worry. I'll be alright and I'll call you in two weeks cause I'm living for me now. No more daddy's little girl, that's all in the past. Thanks," Rhonda said, smiling.

"I want to thank everyone here. You all made it possible for me to get back on my feet. Although I hated this place in the beginning, I've come to love it and respect the people that run it. So thank you all for helping me," she cried.

They all hugged her emotionally and a quietness crept through the corridor as she slowly exited the door, heading for the bus stop. Wanda wanted to surprise her family as she had informed the head of the facility when they asked who she wanted to call. On her ride home, her mind wondered about many things and she knew she had to put things in order the way they were supposed to be in the first place. Therefore, she had pre–planned everything to perfection and she was ready to put them into effect.

Once she got there, she noticed the place was nicely cleaned. She thought that was certainly unusual because she knew those two made messes all the time. After discovering no one home, she decided to sit and relax herself in the Jacuzzi hot tub. Finally, the comforts of home had come upon her as she thought how wonderful it was and how foolish she had been giving it all up. Nevertheless, those days were gone and she was back to stay.

Doug made his way back home and went into the den to study. He eventually nodded off to sleep; never knowing that Wanda was in the house as she relaxed upstairs. After about an hour of hot bubbles, she decided to come out and pamper herself, get dressed and eat something. Upon reaching the kitchen, she noticed an enormous amount of food that normally wouldn't be there. But she dug into it like there was no tomorrow, since she hadn't eaten anything of that sort in a while.

After fixing a large tray of various foods and fruit, she retrieved a pitcher of lemonade and headed for the den. However, she was shocked as she saw Doug asleep on her favorite chair. She placed the tray on the table and took a seat on the sofa, grabbing the remote. As she ate and watched television, she gazed at Doug lying there innocently sleeping.

She wondered how he would respond when he noticed her back home; she couldn't wait to finish eating. However, she couldn't help wondering where Doug Jr. was being that he always stayed close to his dad on Saturdays and Sundays. After Wanda finished eating, she stood and took off her nightgown, grabbed the remote and turned the television all the way up as she stood directly in front of the tube. Suddenly, from the loud sound, Doug awoke, shocked to see her standing there before him.

"When did you get out?" he asked in amazement.

Wanda walked closer and spoke softly, "About three hours ago. I was upstairs relaxing in the tub. I never heard you come in," she said.

"I was tired and fell asleep," he explained.

"Too tired for me?" she asked seductively.

Doug was more than elated to see her, but this wasn't what he had in mind. However, he could never resist her in any way. "I'm never too tired for you. You're always on my mind," he said smoothly.

"Then come on, let's go upstairs and get reacquainted," she told him.

Doug knew what was about to take place and he wasn't quite

ready for it, but had to perform. "Why didn't you inform me before you got out?" he asked her.

"Because I wanted to surprise you," she said softly.

"And that you did my dear," he shot back.

"Where's my son?" she asked as she entered the bedroom.

"He's out with Sonya," he said softly.

"Who is Sonya?" she asked sharply.

"She's the daughter of my therapist, Dr. Williams. She's seventeen, and her and little Doug get along great," he exclaimed, looking in her eyes.

"Oh really?" she shot back.

"By the way, did you hide some money before you left? Doug Jr. found it in some shoe boxes," he asked her.

"Yes! It was yours," she told him.

"What do you mean…it was mine? Where did you get it?" he asked.

"One of your cousin's workers brought it and said he had a lot of heat on him and that he was leaving town. So he handed me the suitcase and took off. But I have to be honest, I spent some of it," she said as she looked innocently in his eyes.

"That's alright. I thought it was yours and I spent some of it too. Now I don't have to replace it, that's good," he shot back.

"Is there anything else you need to tell me that I would need to know. So there won't be any surprises?" she inquired, slipping into bed.

"No… that's all," he said, sliding in beside her.

She looked at him in his eyes and softly planted a kiss on the lips as he took charge and made passionate love to her, something they both had been long awaiting. Later, they lay in bed discussing their plans as he brought her up to date on everything that had taken place in her absence. He avoided the issues he knew would eventually cause more conflict. After showering together and getting dressed, they both decided it would be a good idea to go shopping as Wanda wanted to upgrade her wardrobe. Doug was more than happy to escort her since he didn't want to still be in bed when Sonya and Doug Jr. arrived. However, he left a note to tell them where he was and that Wanda was home. He did this so Sonya wouldn't be caught off guard.

Rita was clearing things to take off for the day, as her salon was full of patrons. She figured she deserved the rest of the day to herself and wanted to find a way to get away from it all. So she left and headed out, hoping she would find something that might excite her. After riding, paying a few bills and enjoying the view, she decided to go pick out a few outfits and see if there was any new fashion out there.

She entered a full mall parking lot. She had trouble finding a parking spot and had to walk a distance. Upon reaching the entrance exhausted, she decided to check out the Gap first for some new apparel. "May I help you with anything today?" A young pretty girl asked nicely.

"I was hoping to find some fashionable jeans that has a maternity elastic," she informed the young girl.

"We have those over there, but you don't look pregnant. I hope I can carry mine and continue looking that good," the young girl said smiling.

"Well, thank you, I just found out and I'm getting ready now for when the time comes this body will change then for sure and I don't want to be caught off guard," Rita stated gracefully.

Smiling, the young girl pointed in the direction of maternity clothes, showing her the latest fashions, as Rita carefully picked through the entire rack slowly.

"If you need any more assistance, call me," the girl stated.

"Thank you, I will," Rita shot back. Rita found numerous outfits to her liking and purchased them all, giving the young girl plenty of work and a generous commission for her efforts. Stocked with three bags, she headed for the next store. Now she needed shoes.

Meanwhile, Doug was frustrated, trying not to show his agitation as Wanda was trying on numerous dresses by designer Ann Taylor. She constantly asked his opinion in which he could've cared less being that she looked good in anything to him. However, he wanted to always please her, but right now he was tired and drained from all his recent experiences with the other women. It had started taking its toll and he knew it had to cease now that she was back home again.

Finally, Wanda was ready, after choosing a few dresses from the designer collection. After purchasing the clothes, they headed out to where Wanda could find shoes for her outfits. Browsing by the Rack room, Wanda spotted something in the window that caught her attention, and decided to go inside and look further, while Doug followed, holding the bags with what she just purchased earlier. As she tried on shoe after shoe, Doug sat patiently imagining how lucky he was meeting her. Then suddenly he looked up and saw Rita coming down the aisle carrying bags.

"Hello," Rita said, approaching Wanda smiling.

"Hi...I see you're overloaded," Wanda said making conversation.

"I guess I got a little over excited," she said as she then noticed Doug sitting there.

"To say the least, if you had any more, you might not be able to carry it all," she shot back.

"I didn't know you even knew where I was," Wanda said.

"Actually, for a while I didn't, but after not seeing you for a while I asked Doug. And he informed me that you went into rehab," she exclaimed.

"Oh, is that right?" she shot back sarcastically.

"Well, I'm happy you're home," Rita exclaimed, having to bite her tongue to get it out.

"Thank you. It will never happen again," she told her.

"That's good. I'm sure it's better having you around," she said. However, Wanda was shocked at her response, knowing she had her eyes on Doug.

"Well, I'm pooped. I need a break," Wanda said.

"Now that's not a bad idea if I must say so myself. Let's get a bite to eat," Doug commented, feeling rather tired from all the shopping. Wanda was in agreement.

"Okay! Do you want to join us Rita?" Wanda asked out of respect, not expecting her to say yes.

"I could use something to eat," she shot back.

Doug was hoping she would decline as he looked at her. Nevertheless, it was too late. Rita had made her way to finding out all she could now. Doug thought to himself about how he could straighten her out later on.

"Let's get a steak sub," Doug suggested. As they gathered in line to order, the young girl assisted them quickly and they all sat at the table in the center square.

"Seems you both went off the deep end," Doug commented, referring to their shopping bags.

"I'm not finished...there's so much more I need," Wanda implied.

"Well, I can't carry all this, but I do need a few more accessories," Rita added.

"I never can understand why you need so many clothes"…Doug said looking at the bags.

"It's a woman thing," Wanda expressed laughing.

Suddenly Rita looked up as she saw Michelle walking towards them smiling. She knew that wasn't a good sign, being that she held a grudge against Doug and her.

"Hello…well isn't this a surprise. I never expected to see the three of you together," Michelle blurted out sarcastically.

"And what brings you here?" Doug asked.

"This is where I work since my boss terminated me and I kinda like the atmosphere," she said cleverly.

Wanda was surprised at the comment, as she sensed the tension in the air. "Well, that's what happens when you're embezzling money," he shouted.

"I somehow don't feel that's the real reason It was more to it and you know it," she shot back angrily.

"Nevertheless, it's over and there's no use dwelling on it anymore. It's not about to change now, so let it go," Doug said loudly.

"I see you think you still have all the answers," she shouted.

"No…but that's the best solution for this one," he shot back.

"What are you going to do about this one?" she said laughing.

"What one," he asked wondering.

"The one you're about to have when Wanda finds out that Rita here is carrying your baby," she said walking away.

"What?" Wanda shouted, looking at Doug for a response…

"Don't listen to her. She's crazy," he said.

"She wouldn't have just made an accusation like that if it didn't have some truth to it," Wanda responded.

"Like I said. She's crazy," he shot back, hoping she wouldn't make a scene.

"And you have a hell of a nerve sitting here innocently as if everything's alright, you dirty winch. I've never trusted you and I always knew you wanted Doug," she exclaimed angrily.

"Well, you don't deserve him, you sorry bitch or you would not have started doing drugs," Rita shot back.

"Okay, that's enough," Doug shouted.

"I don't want to hear nothing you have to say right now. You can't keep your dick in your pants," Wanda shouted.

"If that's the case and you're placing blame, you should've stayed your ass straight, then none of this would've happened. But you're the one that ran off doing cocaine, neglecting your son and everyone else. So you need to check yourself first because it's your fault," Rita shouted.

"Bitch, I'm bout to check you," Wanda said, standing to her feet as Doug stood and held her.

"Hold it…stop," Doug interrupted. "I need to tell you both something that's very important but not here. Let's go to my place. I don't want to hear no more arguing," he told them as they headed to their cars.

Doug knew that he had to reveal their secret before they totally destroyed one another and their chances of ever bonding as sisters. As soon as they arrived, he felt the tension in the air. He was glad Sonya and Doug Jr. hadn't made it back. They gathered in the den waiting for whatever Doug had to tell them.

"This better be good," Wanda blurted.

"The reason I brought you both here is not easy for me to explain and it was rather complex when I first heard about it, so I'm going to cut through the chase. Rita, you and Wanda are sisters."

"What?" They both shouted.

"What the hell are you talking about?" Wanda screamed.

"I know this comes as a shock to you both, but I'm here to tell you, it's true. It wasn't a coincidence that you were put together out of the blue. It was planned and it was meant so you could eventually get to know each other," Doug stated.

"This is crazy. It's impossible," Wanda claimed.

"So why do you think your father really up and left…and hasn't returned?" Doug asked her.

"Because of his job," she shot back.

"That's what your parents wanted you to believe," Doug told her.

"And how do you know all this?" Wanda asked him curiously.

"Your mother," he said.

"What?" she screamed.

"That's right, you heard me. Your mother came by my office and informed me after finding out about me and Rita, telling me the whole story," He said.

"And why would she tell you and not us?" Wanda asked.

"Because she wanted me to leave and not interfere with what she had worked so hard putting together. In other words, she didn't want me involved in either of your lives any longer but the damage had already been done and I couldn't walk away. I know this doesn't dismiss the fact of what happened, but at least now that you both know, you can find ways to tolerate one another and get along," Doug stated.

"It still doesn't make any sense," Rita said looking at them.

"That's because you never knew who your parents were...and your father has passed away. You both have the same mother and Wanda's father was always away from home due to his jobs. Therefore, her... I mean your mother had an affair in which you were the end result. Wanda's father had left her mother and never knew about her being pregnant and when they reconciled, you were sent to stay with a cousin who lead you to believe you were adopted. But she had all intentions of raising you together.

However, things didn't work out in that order, but she kept close tabs on you the whole time and when you grew up to understand, she decided to bring you two together. But it wasn't meant to because Wanda's father wouldn't or couldn't accept the fact that she had gotten pregnant while they were married, even though they were separated at the time. So that's the whole story as it was told to me anyway," Doug stated honestly.

"Now, we must talk to her," Wanda said lowly.

"That would be your best source," Doug suggested.

"When do you want to do that?" Rita asked.

"I don't know, and it still doesn't solve our problem cause. The fact remains you're pregnant by my man," she snapped.

"That's done and we can't change it."

"It's not her fault. I take responsibility for that and I can't desert her now. I can and will uphold my responsibility to my kid. Hopefully you can respect that. If not, then I hate it because I would do the same for you in this situation," Doug stated sharply.

"We'll discuss this later. Right now I'm tired and confused amongst various other things," Wanda said softly.

At that moment, the door opened and Doug Jr. came in with Sonya following him. Surprised to see his mother, he ran straight into her arms. "Mommy, when did you get home?" he asked her happily.

"This morning baby. What you been doing all day? I missed you so much," she said, holding him tightly.

"Me and Sonya been shopping and riding all morning," he said.

"I see…What did you buy?" she asked.

"A bunch of cool stuff. If I would've known you were coming home, I would've bought you a present," he said smiling.

"That's nice…aren't you going to introduce me to your friend?" she asked curious to meet her.

"Yeah…Sonya this is my mother," he said.

"Hello! I heard so much about you He speaks of you often," she said with a smile.

"Hi. How are you? I hope he hasn't been much trouble for you. I know he has his moments," she responded back.

"Sonya, this is Rita and you met Wanda, her sister," Doug said, revealing it to her.

"Hi," she said softly.

"Hello," Rita said in return.

"We both bought you something, here's mine," Sonya said as she handed him the bathrobe.

"Thanks for being considerate," Doug replied.

"I bought you a wallet and money clip, dad," Doug Jr. snapped.

"Thank you, son. Now if I can hold onto something to put in it for a change," Doug said firmly.

"Sonya, how old are you?" Rita asked shyly.

"I'm seventeen. My birthday is next week," she informed her.

"Are you still in school?" she asked her. "I graduated and I'm planning on going to college in the fall," she said.

"Mr. Walsh if you're not going anywhere, I'm going to check on my mother and pick up a few things," she informed him.

"Sure, go ahead. We'll be here," he told her.

"Who is your mother?" Wanda asked out of curiosity.

"Dr. Amy Williams," she said.

"Her mother is my therapist," Doug stated.

"Oh…" Wanda sighed.

"I'll return later," Sonya implied as she gathered her bags and headed for the door.

"Nice girl. Very well mannered," Wanda implied, looking at Doug.

"Yeah, and she take good care of little Doug," he said.

"She's my friend mommy," Doug Jr. added.

"So, how have you been doing in school?" Wanda asked her son.

"Great! Sonya's been helping me," he informed her.

"Seems like she contributes a lot around here," Wanda shot back.

"I'll say, the place is immaculately clean," Rita added.

"Well, I'm back now and we no longer need her services," she said.

"Correction, she's under contract until the fall when she starts school. Her room is booked until then," Doug informed her.

"Her room? She's been staying with you?" Wanda snapped.

"Of course! How else would I have maintained without you?" he said.

Thoughts were running through her head, being she was a young attractive girl with a drop dead figure on her. She wondered if they had been intimate in any way. Nevertheless, time would tell as she planned to watch for the signs.

CHAPTER 16

As Veronica was attempting to clean her place, the doorbell rang. She opened the door and to her surprise there stood Kiana. "Hello…may I come in?" she asked calmly.

"Come on in, Can I get you something?" she asked her.

"No. I first want to say I'm sorry. I hope you forgive me. I was wrong from striking you and I'm here to let you know that I'm not holding any grudges against you," Kiana expressed honestly.

"That's good to know and I accept your apology. However, I was wrong for not telling you about the videotape," she said.

"Speaking of the videotape, that's what I want to discuss with you. I need to know, are those tapes shown here?" Kiana asked.

"Some are and some are only sold abroad," she informed her.

"Abroad?" she asked quickly.

"Yes, but they are hardcore only," she told her.

"How much does one of these pay?" Kiana asked her.

"Why? Are you interested?" she asked her.

"Depends…" she shot back. "How much money will I be making?"

"$10,000.00 and a percentage, if they decide to take the videotape and distribute it abroad, but it's got to be hardcore," she said.

"What kind of hardcore?" Kiana asked.

"A lot of freaky shit, you know. Butt fucking or anything beyond the normal. People love seeing someone licking ass," she said to her.

"I got another female and my husband willing to participate."

"That's double if I join in, if that's alright with you. We can get paid within a week after we finish it," she informed her.

"Sounds good. I was hoping you would be a part of it. Set it up, I'll go tell them. When can we start?" Kiana asked her.

"Tonight, if that's alright with you," she informed her.

"Good…" Kiana said as she hugged and kissed her. "Friends?"

"Sure," Veronica responded.

U. E. Wynn

"I'll see you later," she said as she left smiling.

Veronica went to her phone and set up for the taping, knowing she was about to make a lot more for her commission and for participating in the video. Now she could stay put and make a life for herself, instead of running here and there as she had been doing for the past year.

Meanwhile, Kiana had addressed Tenita about the prospect of getting paid as they had their fling together, as she was in total agreement with the chance to showcase her and convince her husband about the hardcore action. This was something he hadn't experienced and she wasn't sure he would even respond to the idea. However, she had planned on convincing him quickly cause they needed a male. It was either him or they would have to find someone else, the show was already set. Before dark, Kiana had solved her problem with the help of Tenita and they were packed and on their way.

Doug had finally gotten things under control and took off, heading for Dr. Williams's house, wondering why Sonya hadn't made her way back.

"Hello! To what do I owe the pleasure?" she said upon answering the door.

"Hello Amy, I was wondering, did Sonya come over here? She said she would return. I was concerned," Doug implied.

"She came by and stayed a little while before she took off in her new car," she said comically.

"Good, now I'm relieved," Doug stated.

"Please come in. I missed you," she told him.

"I thought of you a lot too," he said.

"Let's cut to the chase. You know what I want…and what you need," she said softly. They headed upstairs to the bedroom, where she quickly undressed him and engaged in some vigorous sex. Doug informed her he couldn't stay long and quickly dressed as the contents of his pants pockets spilled to the floor. He retrieved his belongings and he left, heading for home. As he returned home, he noticed Rita had left and Sonya had returned, eager to take care of things as she was cleaning her closet and placing her clothes in order.

"Oh, I see you're back. I went over to your mother's looking for you," he told her.

"I told her I was coming back, but I changed my mind," she said.

"I hope you're still going to be here since Wanda is back," he asked her.

"I'm sure things will be alright, she doesn't seem to be a bad person. I would be concerned too…so she had a good reason. I don't fault her for being protective or being somewhat insecure," she said as she rubbed her hand up his leg.

"We must be very careful," he informed her.

"Don't worry, I will," she said, winking her eye. "I'm going to watch a movie with little Doug. You want to watch it with me?" she asked him.

"I'm going to pass. I have to discuss a few things with Wanda," he said.

"Alright! Just save some for me," she said and kissed him before he headed to his room.

Wanda was furious and rather sexual as she waited for Doug to enter the room. He noticed her lying across the bed on her stomach, her pretty brown round ass standing out above her back looking good. He knew what he had to do and was ready for the task.

"We need to talk," she said as he entered the room.

"I know, but that's going to have to wait," he said as he rubbed her smooth legs until her senses eased upon his hand reaching her big round ass, spoke all she needed.

As Kiana and her husband entered the bedroom, Tenita noticed Veronica playing with a dildo, vibrating it in her pussy. The excitement enticed her automatically to where she wasted no time getting undressed as the video camera was visible and rolling. She looked at Kiana, who had followed suit, lying beside her, taking the vibrator, pushing it deeper and deeper as she moaned. Tenita sucked her firm breast and squeezed hard, enhancing her pleasure as though she knew what she wanted. Kiana was on her knees pushing the vibrator in and out of Veronica with her ass in the air as her husband watched in excitement. He approached Kiana from behind, entering her and thrusting his dick to the hilt. This action disrupted her motion with the vibrator. Veronica then took the vibrator out of her pussy and stuck it in Kiana's mouth as her husband pounded her from behind. Tenita sat up and slid under Kiana, licking her pussy as her husband's dick went in and out.

However, Veronica pulled the dildo out of her mouth and stuck it in Tenita. Lying under her, Kiana screamed loud as she climaxed in

Tenita's face from the force of her husband pounding hard. He then pulled out and stuck his dick in Tenita's mouth as she sucked hard while Veronica teased her clit with the dildo. Kiana spread Veronica's legs and began licking her clit while she teased Tenita, losing focus from the sensitive tongue driving her nuts. She climaxed quickly, spurting her juices over Kiana's face with a powerful burst.

She then took the dildo and stuck it in her mouth, moistening it with her saliva as she stood and put Kiana on her knees. She pushed her head between Tenita's legs, inviting her to enjoy herself. She gently pushed the dildo up her ass slowly until she buried it. Kiana yelled loud in pleasure as she stroked in and out of her butt with the large object, feeling as though she had been split.

She gradually reared back and forth to meet the thrust of the dildo. Kiana grabbed her husband's dick and sucked it while the dildo was being pushed into her ass, increasing her pleasure as Tenita was now under Veronica, eating away. Veronica instructed him to come put his dick in Tenita's ass, being the camera was set-up with a direct shot of her ass. The minute he entered her, she screamed louder as he pushed in and out vigorously, making slurping noises with each stroke.

She suddenly climaxed hard, screaming loud as she collapsed on the bed. Veronica turned around and pushed it up in her, meeting his thrust as hard as she could and reaching a quick orgasm. Kiana wasn't about to miss out and turned around as he plunged deep into her with a vengeance. Surprised, he had so much staying power, she gracefully took all he had up in her as he pushed it deep in her ass and exploded. They all collapsed on the bed, the show was over. The video was complete and they were more satisfied from the pleasure they all received. Veronica explained the details of their money, which they all agreed to.

Doug Jr. had fallen asleep on the sofa as the movie ended. Sonya picked him up and carried him to the room and put him to bed. As she headed for her room, she could hear moans of passion from the master bedroom and imagined the pleasure Wanda was receiving from Doug, something she was destined to experience again herself real soon. She continued on to her room for the night.

The next morning she woke early, before anyone got up and headed home to her mother, where she had forgotten a few things. "Hi mom," she said entering the house.

"Sonya, Doug came by looking for you," her mom said.

"Yes, he told me last night. I had to come pick up some of my things," she said.

"It seems we don't see much of each other now," her mom said, hoping to receive a positive response.

"Oh, do you miss me Ma?" she asked laughing.

"You know I miss having you around. You're all I got. I love you sweetheart," her mom expressed sincerely.

"I love you too. Don't worry, we'll spend some time together soon cause Doug Jr.'s mother is home now and I'm going to college this fall. They won't need me around, so I'll be staying home," she said.

"That's good. Oh, you left your cell phone. It's in my room on the dresser," she informed her.

Sonya retrieved her things and headed into her mother's bedroom, where the cell phone sat on top of the dresser. Upon picking up the phone, she noticed the money clip by the head of the bed and knew Doug had been in the bedroom. Was he sleeping with her mother? She thought furiously as she hoped she was wrong.

"Mom, I'm leaving. I'll see you later," she told her.

"Okay, take care and tell Doug hello for me. And he doesn't have to remain a stranger."

"Okay, love you," she said, exiting the house mad as she believed he was sleeping with her mom from the statement she made. She thought about how she would confront Doug as she drove back to the estate. However, she dismissed the thought and decided to see how he would respond to her finding the money clip in her mother's bedroom. Somehow she knew things were about to change real soon.

Wanda had made her way over to talk to her mother.

"Mom, why didn't you tell me about Rita?" she asked.

"I see you have been talking to Doug. Things got out of hand when your father and I split up. I got pregnant and tried to keep it hidden until I could manage telling him. I never meant for anyone to get hurt by it, but I couldn't control it any longer as it was eating at me constantly. After your father rejected it, I had to find a way to get you both together and that was the best way I knew how. So I connected you without your knowledge, hoping you would become friends, for me to tell you about it," she said.

"Why didn't you just come straight out and tell us?" she asked.

"Because I feared it would do more harm than good, since things had already fallen apart with your father and me. Losing another one of you would've crushed me to the point I would've fell apart. The pressure was enormous and I couldn't take much more. I was a wreck," she explained.

"Now I'm confused," Wanda stated slowly.

"About what honey?" Her mother asked.

"How I should accept her?" she said.

"Just simply love her, she's your family," she informed her.

"It's not that simple now," she shot back.

"Why not?" she asked.

"Because she's pregnant by Doug," she told her.

"What? That's no good," she blurted.

"It happened before he knew. I can't place all the blame upon him. She had intentions from the start to do this," she explained.

"I don't know what to say. I really don't know," she said slowly.

"There's nothing you can say. I'll just have to live with it, cause what's done is done," Wanda said softly.

"Don't hold it against her. It'll only destroy both of you, and defeat the purpose of my bringing you both together, which I hope you want to do," she told her.

"I'm not going to hold a grudge, but trust isn't going to come easy. She'll have to earn it," she said bluntly.

"That's understandable, just give her a chance," she told her.

"I will. Take care, I'll see you later," she said leaving. Cassandra was studying in the library, hoping she could occupy her mind to get things in prospective, being that she was distraught over what happened recently. But this wasn't going to disturb her to the point where she would fall apart, even though she couldn't stop thinking about it by any means. Her life had to go with or without her family and friends, although she needed the comfort of being loved and wanted as everyone else.

"Hello, my name is Karen Wittmore. I noticed you over here on the computer and I was wondering if you have any knowledge of setting up a website?" The woman asked.

"Actually, I don't but I'm sure someone here can assist you in some way," she responded, wondering why she wanted a website. Cassandra knew she was a substitute teacher recently employed by the school.

"Thank you, I'm new here and it's going to take a while for me to find my way around," the woman said.

"I'm sorry. I wish I could've been of some help to you," she told her.

"That's alright. Sometimes it's better to start from the end to the beginning," the woman exclaimed walking away.

Cassandra was baffled by the comment as she meditated on what the woman said leaving. She felt so much alive to the reality of life. Now she had to discover its true meaning before she could be content with her ordeal. Nevertheless, the fact she would have to contact the ones that she had the confrontation with scared her and she couldn't get up enough nerve to face them right now. But that would be the only way to solve the problem, by going directly to the source. Her family would be more receptive to it. But how she could ever face Doug in this situation was what presented the biggest problem. However, she had to find a way.

Alicia was on her lunch break heading to get a bite to eat. Upon pulling into the drive-through, she ordered quickly, hoping to hurry back to work. After receiving her order, she pulled out, heading back to work when she noticed Calvin driving along in front of her with a female passenger in the car. She followed from a distant, distinctively undetected, until he made a turn into the drug store where she observed his baby's mama exit the car. Looking closely, she noticed she was pregnant. Shocked, she wondered if the baby might be Calvin's. She decided he needed to at least see her without making a scene. So she quickly drove past and acknowledged him with her and continued on to work. She knew she would either receive a call or confront him about it tonight. Meanwhile, he had some explaining to do.

Doug sat in his study pondering his thoughts as his fax sent his quarterly earnings. He noticed a slight increase, which was an enormous profit. Suddenly he reached for the phone.

"Hello, Bank of America," the voice answered.

"I guess I owe you some kind of commission," he said smoothly.

"Excuse me?" the voice responded.

"My earnings have increased graciously," he repeated.

"Doug, is that you?" the voice said.

"Who else were you expecting?" he responded.

"It took me a while to catch your voice," she said softly.

"I just received the fax of my quarterly earnings and I figured that

I owe you one," he said.

"That's funny. I don't know why cause I didn't send any fax," she said sternly.

"I thought it came from you," he said.

"Nope, not me," Yvonne stated.

"Then it must be from my accountant," he said.

"I guess that's who you owe the commission to. I only make sure nothing is transferred out of your name," she stated.

"I'll have to contact her later. So what's been going on with you?" he asked her.

"I'm holding on and keeping things in perspective, hoping to advance in any way I can right now," she informed him.

"If I know you, then you'll find a way," he said.

"I heard you been through quite some excitement," she said.

"And where did you hear that?" he asked.

"Cassandra. She wants to talk to you, but she's not sure how you're going to respond, since what happened," she informed him.

"I don't hold grudges. Why would she think that?" he asked.

"I think she's afraid. That's just her, call her. I'm sure she wants to hear from you," she insisted.

"Right now might not be a good time," he said.

"Why not?" she asked curiously.

"Wanda is back home, and that may create a problem," he said.

Oh, I see. Well, take care and I'll holla at you later," she said.

"Sure thing," he said.

Yvonne couldn't wait to inform Cassandra about what she had just learned and phoned her.

"Hello," Cassandra answered. "I just talked with Doug and he informed me after I told him you wanted to call him," she said before being interrupted.

"You did what? Why?" Cassandra yelled.

"Girl chill, he said he didn't hold grudges, giving me the indication he would love to hear from you. Although he did say it might create a problem right now," she told her.

"What do you mean by that?" Cassandra asked her.

"He told me Wanda was back home," she shot back. "That's his son's mother, she was in rehab," she told her.

"I see," she said softly.

"So are you going to call him?" Yvonne asked interested.

"I will, eventually," Cassandra responded.

"Alright, I'll talk to you later," she shot back.

"Okay!" she responded and hung up the phone.

Wanda came into the study, looked Doug in the eyes and asked him, "Do you really love me?"

"Hell yeah!" He responded hastily.

"I mean, are you in love with me?" she repeated.

"Of course I am! Why you ask me that?" he replied.

"Because there's a difference between the two that most people don't understand the significance. I need to know because if you really love me, I mean in love with me, then you shouldn't hesitate on my next question," she told him.

"What's the question because I'm in love with you and I'll do whatever I can to see you happy," he responded.

"Marry me!" She said sternly.

"I was going to do that anyway," he said standing.

"No, I mean right now, set a date and lets get married or we need to go our separate ways. There's been so much drama and I can't continue doing this," she said seriously.

"Okay, you set the date," he told her.

"Around Christmas would be fine, and I want you to throw an engagement party telling everyone so that we erase any doubts about whom we are devoted to," she informed him.

"Okay, it's done. Anything else?" he asked her.

"Invite everyone, don't leave out nobody. I mean past flames and all, I want them all there to hear it," she said angrily.

"Alright my love," he said softly in her ear.

"So how does it feel being my husband?" she asked.

"Great," he said, smiling.

Doug knew she had him against the wall and he had to meet her demands at any cost since she was the only woman that could totally destroy him at the drop of a dime. Nevertheless, it was always his intention to marry her anyway. But now she was forcing his hand to the limit and he had to take action and produce, regardless. Besides, he really loved her.

Cassandra pondered about how she would confront Doug and explain how she went about things in the wrong way. However, she had no idea her efforts now would be to no avail. She had waited too late.

U. E. Wynn

CHAPTER 17

Wanda was highly motivated, making all sorts of arrangements for she had high hopes and expected everything to turn out perfect on her wedding day. She got fitted for her wedding dress, arranged the setting and informed the pastor, all in the same day. However, she wasn't revealing it to anyone in particular. She wanted to see how Doug would handle that end of the deal. Therefore, she even kept it from her mother, opting to make out the invitations for things to run smooth. Besides, she wasn't about to let anyone ruin it under any circumstances.

Meanwhile, Doug had come up with a plan of his own and hoped it would meet her standards, as he was sure it would be exciting, to say the least. Once he set it up, it would be large and everyone would have a good time and enjoy themselves.

"Hello, I'm glad I caught you. I have a proposition for you and Mimi, and I think you'll agree that's very profitable for both of you," he said.

"What is it Doug?" she asked hurriedly.

"I don't want this out right now. So I have to have your promise you won't mention it to anyone just yet, cause I don't want everyone prying into my business, creating more problems," he informed her. Doug wasn't convinced by the sound of her voice and decided against telling her it was an engagement party. "I want to rent your club on Halloween night and throw a nice party, I mean big," he said.

"Sounds good, we're not booked. Who do you want to perform?" she asked him.

"I'll cover that end; I just want to be assured you're in agreement and provide me access!" He told her.

"Of course…it's all yours. I'll tell Mimi and then whatever you want us to do, we'll handle it," she said.

"That's what I wanted to hear. I'll get back to you and we can get the price straightened out," he informed her.

"Good!" she responded.

Doug explained his plan to Wanda and she thought it was a great way to break the news. However, she felt it would be better if he assisted her to tell her mother cause she wasn't coming to a party under any circumstances. She felt she needed to be the first one they told about the wedding. Doug agreed and asked her when she wanted to give her the news, hoping she would say right away to get it over with since he didn't like his last encounter with her. Hopefully, this would give her a change of heart to accept him. They decided no time is better than the present and headed her way.

Yvonne confirmed to Mimi what Doug had planned, letting her know that he wanted to preserve the club Halloween night for the party and that they would provide everything needed since he was planning something special for the event. They both were overwhelmed and looked forward to it, being that it was only two weeks away.

Calvin came in that evening unaware that Alicia was really upset about the incident she saw earlier that day.

"Did you have a nice time today?" she asked him.

"Don't start...I'm not in the mood," he informed her.

"So you think I'm not to be concerned about you messing around on me?" she shot back.

"What are you talking about? I was only taking her to get some prescriptions filled for my son," he told her. "What? I can't spend time with my son now?" he said.

"I noticed she's pregnant also," she replied.

"So what?" he shot back.

"Is it yours?" she asked him.

"Why are you asking all these questions?" he said abruptly.

"I take it that's a yes?" she said evilly.

"I'm not married to you. What makes you think I have to answer to you?" he asked her.

"Our relationship is based on honesty, truth and faithfulness, but you don't seem to understand that or even care," she informed him.

"I'm not jumping at your every whim. You think it's all about you, but the world doesn't revolve around you. So act like you know," he said as he stormed out the door.

Alicia then realized he had no intentions of being faithful and he wasn't about to change. She was furious at his actions.

Doug was glad that was over and he could finally start making preparations for the party. He started making phone calls for someone to perform for the event. He wanted to make it look as though it was your basic Halloween party and in the process reveal that he was about to get married, instead of announcing it was an engagement party.

He needed a big name to draw the people in for it. So he decided to call in some favors and make some contacts to pull it off. However, he knew he would have to get lucky, since he was doing it at the spur of the moment and the chances everyone wasn't already booked was going to be slim to none. Nevertheless, he had to push his hand and hope that he could find someone to do the show. While he had that in motion, he asked Wanda about who she wanted to invite. They both sat making out invitations for the event, informing their guest they must wear costumes, as they both had guests that they didn't want the other to know about. It was sure to be a good night, full of fun and excitement.

Now they had to figure out what they were going as. Wanda suggested they wear something that matched. However, Doug wasn't in agreement with the idea. He suggested that they wear Batman and Cat-woman suits. Wanda agreed that was close enough. They hurried and put the invitations in the mail, hoping everyone had enough time to attend the event. Sonya entered and asked what was going on, noticing a table full of cards.

"We're throwing a Halloween party," Wanda informed her smiling widely.

"Of course... sounds like fun," she replied.

"You have to be in costume," she implied.

"No problem," she said quickly.

"Then here's your invitation," Wanda said, handing her the card from the table already written out.

"Thanks," she responded. Doug noticed she had already planned on inviting her as the card was already written out with her name on it. Things were quickly falling into place as planned by day's end; hopefully everything would go smoothly, being they were rushing into the event rather hastily.

Meanwhile, Wanda had a plan of her own that was sure to cause havoc on its own, amongst his female friends. She knew once Rita found out about the wedding, it would create problems and Doug would have to answer for it. As she already knew, he was trying desperately not to let anyone find out before time. She had to disrupt his plan and make him reveal to them all who he really loved and was choosing to be with, giving her the satisfaction and respect she felt she deserved, after being somewhat humiliated.

Unaware of her plan, Doug sent out the invitations, not knowing she had revealed the wedding only to certain ones. Doug was informed the next day that George Clinton was available to perform at the event. However, that wasn't who he had in mind, but he always wore his costume which made it that much more appropriate for him to headline. Now it was time to get things set up at the club, while he could catch Yvonne and Mimi before they did anything out of the ordinary for the event.

"Hello. I'm glad I caught you before you left," he said.

"We practically live in here," Mimi replied.

"So what's going on?" Yvonne asked.

"I've got George Clinton to perform…so we're going to need a light show and plenty of room around the stage," he replied.

"Then we need a lot of work done," Mimi said.

"On the contrary, we don't. I've already made arrangement for the electrician to come and install what we need…but there's one problem," he said bluntly.

"What's that?" Yvonne implied.

"The work he does will be permanent," he said.

"And you think that's a problem?" she shot back.

"Good!"

"I'm glad you're in agreement, plus you're inheriting about ten thousand dollars' worth of lightning from me with fog and smoke bombs," he told her.

"Sounds good!" They both said, happy to receive the gift.

"Hopefully you both can agree on another ten for renting the club," he informed them. They looked at one another in awe after hearing what they would receive.

"That's fine. What do you think Yvonne?" Mimi asked her.

"Great!" she responded.

"It's going to be a good night," Doug said smiling.

"I would think so at twenty thousand," Mimi responded.

"Actually, it's going to be about fifty when it's over. I'm giving

George his fee up front and catering food, plus you get the profiton all the drinks you sell. I figure, if they want to drink they can pay for their own. I'm supplying everything else, and there's no cover charge at the door," he told them.

"That's fair enough," Yvonne said.

"Good, then we're all set. The lights will be installed first thing in the morning. Can you have someone here to let them in around 8:00?" he asked.

"Sure, no problem…I'll be here," Mimi responded.

"Then we're straight. I'll holla at you later," he said leaving. Upon his travel home, his phone rang. "Hello," he answered.

"I can't believe you would do this to me after what I revealed to you about being honest," Rita screamed.

"What are you talking about?" he asked her.

"Don't play with me, you know damn well what I'm talking about. I received your invitation today to the engagement party," she said angrily.

Doug was shocked as he thought it had to be Wanda who sent the cards out revealing the wedding. "Can we talk about this later?" Doug snapped.

"What's wrong with right now?" she shot back.

"I'll come by and discuss it. I've got to make a stop," he said, knowing he had no intentions of going over there. He was furious, wondering how many others knew.

Doug drove along wondering who else was aware of it. He couldn't wait to see Wanda and find out. However, she only informed three people of the engagement. Nevertheless, they were enough to do the damage and thus far it was working to her advantage. When Doug arrived at the estate, he encountered Sonya and his son outside by the pool.

"Congratulations," Sonya told him. That only made matters worse, making him feel as though everyone knew.

"Thank you," he responded.

"Dad, can I ride my go cart?" Little Doug asked.

"Be careful and remember what I told you…and where's your mother?" he asked.

"She's upstairs in bed," he responded.

"Wanda!" Doug hollered going upstairs.

"Yes!" She responded from the bedroom.

"Why did you reveal the wedding?" he asked angrily.

"Isn't it obvious?" she responded.

"It's supposed to be a surprise," he said.

"It still is a surprise," she told him smiling.

"But you had to let Rita know, huh?" he asked her.

"Does that create a problem? She's my sister, remember, and I felt she should know, so what's the big deal?" she asked.

"I didn't want anyone to know about it," he informed her.

"Well, don't worry, she isn't going to tell anyone," Wanda said knowing her plan worked.

"The least you could've done was discuss it with me," he told her.

"I'm sorry, I thought it was alright," she said.

Doug headed for the office, dismissing the thought of what happened since the damage was done. Veronica got a call from Kiana informing her about the wedding as they talked about the party. Kiana also informed Alicia, who then informed Cassandra, who called Yvonne to find out what she knew.

"Hello," she answered.

"Do you know anything about the engagement party?" she asked curiously.

"What?" she shot back.

"I just got word from Kiana that Doug is getting married, and that he's throwing an engagement party at your club. However, my invitation says a Halloween bash," she informed her.

"That's all he told me. He never mentioned anything about a wedding or engagement party," Yvonne responded. "I thought you weren't interested in him?" she asked.

"A part of me doesn't seem to want to let go," she told her.

"Then listen to your heart girl," she shot back. She decided to find out for herself.

"Hello," he answered.

"Hello, I received your invitation," she informed him. Shocked to hear from her, he wondered if she knew too, since the secret was out already.

"Good, I look forward to seeing you," he responded.

"Is it true?" she asked.

"I guess you've heard like everyone else I suppose," he said.

"Well is it?" she repeated.

"Yes!" He informed her.

"That was all of a sudden…don't you think?" she said.

"Not really…actually it was planned a long time ago, however, it was disrupted by mishap later on," he explained.

"Why didn't you ever reveal her to me?" Cassandra asked him.

"I never felt the need since it never fully developed," he told her.

"So are you truly in love with her?" she asked him.

"Yes! Just as I was with you," he said seriously.

"But you were never truly in love with me," she said.

"What makes you sure?" he asked her.

"Because you would've never slept around, not to mention with my sister," she informed him.

"That was circumstantial and I was clearly a victim of circumstances," he told her.

"But you made the choice on your own," she said.

"I'm entitled to a mistake aren't I?" he said looking at her.

"We all make them; however, we're supposed to make exceptions in some cases," she said.

"I can respect that, but we're also supposed to be forgivers," he said.

"I do forgive you," she shot back.

"I think it's a little late, don't you?" he said.

"Maybe, but you still have time to change your mind," she said.

"That I do, but it's not likely to happen," he told her.

"What if you were convinced?" she shot back seductively.

"I guess that could happen," he said.

"Then meet me," she said.

"I can't right now. I have important business," he lied; fully aware of her intentions and rejecting them instantly.

"Alright," she said, hanging up.

Doug knew he wasn't about to back out of the wedding and she couldn't entice him in no way. However, he did want to create some magic between them one last time since he really did love her. On the other hand, he felt that there was no need to stir up the old emotions and create any more conflict. Besides, he had enough drama in his life and their fling was over as far as he was concerned. Doug had all intentions of settling down with the woman of his dreams and raising the family he always wanted in life.

U. E. Wynn

CHAPTER 18

Mike had been with Doug all day as they put everything in place for the event. Tonight was sure to be remembered for a long time, as they planned on making it memorable for years to come. Doug had dropped little Doug over at his grandmother's house and headed to the estate to pick up Wanda, where Mike had left his car and planned on changing into his Robin costume, so that he could provide the music. They hurriedly got ready and made it there before the crowds started rolling in to make sure things were in order. The sound stage was being set up to perfection as they knew George Clinton and his funk All-Stars preferred it. Now all they had to do was wait for the caterers to bring the enormous load of food ordered to the event.

"Seems everything is going as planned," Doug said to Yvonne.

"Just like you planned it thus far. Hopefully it takes off without a hitch," she expressed joyfully.

"I'm sure it will now. The caterers just pulled in the back, how much food did you order?" Mimi asked Doug.

"Quite a bit, and a variety of everything," he laughed. Doug looked around for Wanda, who had lingered behind and hadn't come in yet.

"Doug, I got a call from Cassandra informing me she heard this was an engagement party, is it true?" Yvonne asked him.

"Yes, but don't reveal it, everyone doesn't know about it," he said. Suddenly Wanda walked in and caught a glimpse of Doug and headed in his direction.

"Hi baby, is everything in order?' She asked.

"So far, let me introduce you to Yvonne and Mimi, the owners of the club," he said.

"Hello," she said, smiling as though her outfit was too tight.

"Hi, how are you?" Mimi said.

"Hello, I'm Yvonne, it's nice to meet you," she said.

"I hope you're hungry, cause there's a boat load of food that we're going to have to get rid of tonight," he said looking at Wanda.

"I'm sure there won't be any left when it's over," she responded.

Doug noticed the caterers set up rather quickly and not a minute too soon. He also noticed George Clinton and his crew pull up behind them and started unloading. Mimi and Yvonne showed them to their dressing rooms, which had been renovated just for the occasion, to suit their taste.

As the crowds begin pouring in slowly, everyone in costume, some could be identified and others couldn't, which kept you in suspense of who they actually were. Doug stood back and noticed Rita came as a wicked witch. Kiana was dressed as a seductress with a tight laced outfit. Alicia was looking innocent as Shirley Temple, curly hair and all. Calvin was Peter Pan and Cassandra's husband showed up dressed as the devil. Mickey was the scarecrow. Dr. Williams was dressed as Cinderella. Tenita's husband was Robin Hood, Veronica was dressed as Wonder Woman, and Kiana's husband was the incredible Hulk. Cassandra came as Orphan Annie, while Tenita was dressed as Betty Boop. Sonya was very creative, dressed as Pippy Longstocking, but the surprise was seeing Michelle in a blonde wig dressed as Marilyn Monroe. Wanda had the sexiest outfit with her skintight leather suit dressed as Cat Woman and Doug followed her as Batman. Mimi was Zena and Yvonne was incognito to everyone, but those close to her.

Mike quickly started everyone partying as he played the latest hits, blaring through the magnificent sound system that had been installed especially for the event. They all hit the dance floor, the crowd was now enormous and more than they expected, since each guest brought a guest of their own. Kiana was on stage dancing to represent her outfit, moving seductively to music, and all eyes were on her as if she was a stripper.

"Will you look at your sister?" Tenita told Alicia.

"That's just how she likes to party. I'm used to it now, and I'm about to join her," Alicia responded, heading her way.

Suddenly, Wanda noticed an older woman approach Doug, she then moved closer.

"Well, Mr. Walsh, I see you don't hesitate when it comes to having a good time," Dr. Williams said smiling with her elegant white dress portraying Cinderella.

"I'm glad you could attend, how are you?" he responded.

"I'm great, it's nothing like letting off stress," She said.

"Mother! I never knew you had that dress," Sonya exclaimed.

"I had it stored away, and I never knew you had such long ponytails either," She said laughing.

"Oh, you got jokes?" Sonya shot back.

"I love you too," She said nagging her daughter.

"So this is your mother?" Wanda asked Sonya.

"Yes, mother, this is Wanda, Doug's wife to be," She said. "Hello, nice to meet you, you've found a fine young man here. Hold onto him," She said.

"Thank you, I will try. I heard a lot about you," Wanda responded.

"Careful, I could take that many ways. You know how some people talk about shrinks," She said smiling.

"I assure you it wasn't bad," Wanda responded.

"That's good. I wouldn't want someone else making a bad impression on me," she shot back.

"Doug, you care to dance?" Sonya asked.

"Sure, let's go!" He responded.

As they headed for the dance floor, Wanda and Dr. Williams continued in conversation while watching them on the dance floor. After everyone was in the groove of things, Doug prepared to announce the entertainment headliner; George Clinton and the P-Funk All-Stars.

The crowd roared as they appeared in costumes of their own, starting the show with one of their classics, *Flashlight.* Suddenly, everyone was up on their feet, rushing the stage as they rocked the house.

Kiana spotted Mimi and kept a close eye on her for the chance to engage in conversation. She hoped to finish what they started the last time they were together. Michelle sat silently at her table observing everyone as they mingled about, not wanting to be noticed. However, her outfit made her visible to everyone that knew her, being that the blonde wig glowed under the lights. However, Yvonne sat and watched them all as if she was in a zone, wondering what's going on. After the group played a melody of their hits, they retired and took a break, promising the crowd more later on when they returned.

Mike took over once again, keeping the crowd on their feet, as he stuck his homemade CD in, continuously playing hit after hit; he tootook a break~ ~ ~ ~. "Now if I didn't know better, I would think you were someone else," he told Yvonne.

"And why is that?" she asked him.

"Because you look exquisite tonight," he responded.

"Well, thank you," she said.

"Can a brother get some play?" he asked her.

"I don't think so," she informed him.

"Are you seeing someone now?" he asked.

"I guess you could say that," she responded.

"Hey guys, what's going on?" Kiana asked while walking up.

"Nothing much, you enjoying yourself?" Yvonne asked, glad that she interrupted their conversation.

"Lovely, just lovely," she shot back.

"Hey Kiana, I haven't seen you in a while," Mike said as he smiled.

"I was wondering when I would see you also," she said.

"Let's catch up on old times," he said taking her hand.

"How are you doing Cassandra?" Doug said as he sat beside her.

"Just fine, now that I'm in your presence," She said smiling.

"I've been meaning to call you. But I've been so busy here lately, I haven't had the chance," he said.

"I can see why, looking around here," she replied.

"I see you two finally found one another," Yvonne implied.

"Hey girl, how're you doing?" Cassandra asked happy to see her.

"I've been making it. It wasn't easy preparing all of this," she shot back.

"Actually, he did most of it," she responded.

"Now she's the one who deserves most of the credit," Doug stated.

"But you're the mastermind," she responded.

"Isn't this a coincidence?" Michelle stated, as she turned around to face them.

"I would say," Doug responded in return as he noticed who she was.

"I was surprised that I received an invitation," she said.

"That makes two of us, I guess you can thank Wanda for inviting you," Doug informed her.

"Cassandra, may I talk with you?" her husband asked, startling everyone at the table.

"Sure...what is it?" she responded.

"I mean privately," he said.

"Excuse me everyone…I'll be back," she informed them.

Suddenly everything went quiet as Cassandra exited the table. "I wonder what that's all about," Yvonne implied.

"I don't know, but keep an eye on her," Doug insisted.

"Alright!" she responded. The bands last set was over and George Clinton called Doug to the stage, informing everyone he had an announcement to make. Doug was hesitant as he was concerned about Cassandra and her husband, who seemed a little touchy. However, he decided it would be a good time to inform everyone of his wedding to Wanda.

He gracefully took the stage and thanked Clinton and his band for performing on such short notice. "I hope you all are having a good time, as it enlightens me to see people happy and having fun. Therefore, I was more than happy to provide the festivities for tonight. And I want to thank you all for coming and making this one memorable night, being this is where I wanted to announce my engagement to Wanda McDonald, who is out there somewhere. Wanda, where are you…come up here."

As Wanda made her way to the stage, "This is something sacred to me and I can't think of anyone that I want to have this ring other than you at this point. I pray that we can have many magical moments together for years to come. Will you marry me?" he asked, looking in her eyes.

"Yes!" she said, accepting the ring of his mother, as he placed it upon her finger and kissed her.

The crowd roared loud with applause as the people gathered closer talking about the surprise. Wanda was elated as she finally received what she wanted in front of a host of his friends and her friends, while many felt angered and somewhat disappointed that it wasn't them on the receiving end.

Rita was sitting with mixed emotions, as Veronica sat furious. Sonya looked on happy for them both, since she knew she would have her way eventually, as it didn't interfere with her plans. Dr. Williams figured all was fine, she had her way and probably could get other chances later, as he still visited her two or three times a month. Cassandra came back in and caught the last of it. She wished him the best, hiding her true feelings as best she possibly could.

Everyone graciously thanked and congratulated the couple as they mingled through the crowd. Mike played Larry Graham's "Just be my Lady" for the two of them as they were glued together, dancing slowly and kissing one another. Then suddenly while they were dancing on the stage they were interrupted by Michelle holding a piece of paper in her hand smiling widely. They stopped abruptly.

"I hate to rain on your parade… but I wouldn't think about living happily ever after just yet. There's a little problem you're going to have," she told them.

"And what's that?" Doug asked.

"I'm sorry… but you can't get married," she informed them.

"What the hell are you talking about?" Wanda screamed as others around heard the conversation.

"I know it's heartbreaking," Michelle said, handing her the paper she was holding. Wanda hurried into the light and read the paper indicating a marriage license with her and Doug's name upon it stating they were married.

"What the hell is this?" she screamed.

"That's what bonds us together for life. And it prevents you or anyone else to even think about getting too close, my dear," she stated.

"Let me see that," Doug stated.

"Oh… It's legit and legal," Michelle said.

"Where did this come from?" Doug asked. "I can't believe you don't remember signing it," she said.

"You no good bitch," he hollered.

"Don't be so hasty. You can buy it from me," she said.

"Buy it from you?" Wanda screamed loud.

"Of course $250,000 isn't too much," she informed her.

"What?" Doug screamed.

"What we got for you right now, you might want to start running away from here quickly," Wanda told her.

"Such violent natured girl you have here," Michelle said sarcastically. "Let me know when you decide and you know how to contact me. By the way, you can keep that copy to assist inyour decision. I have plenty more where that came from," she said laughing. When suddenly two shots rang out and hit her square in the chest area, slamming her to the floor like a thud. The crowd screamed as they saw a figure behind the stage appear and run out the back way.

However, although they all saw the figure, its' face was covered with a mask. As the people were in an uproar, the lights came on and everyone viewed Michelle laying dead. They all saw who shot her, but no one knew who was behind the mask. As the police quickly arrived, no one was allowed to leave, and they were all held for questioning. The police sought to find out who murdered the woman in front of such a large crowd. And the motive behind the killing as it was done out in the opening of a nightclub. They all were in shock and the investigation ruled everyone a suspect, even though they all knew it was no one present at the club. They were determined to find some answers as they knew someone was aware of something. Therefore, Doug told the detectives exactly what had taken place.

As the police asked questions, everyone's story coincided with the others just as it happened, leading the detectives to believe that they were in fact telling the truth. After everyone was questioned separately, they were allowed to leave at the end of the night, with the warning they can be considered a suspect and be called in for more questioning at any given time until this case is solved andclosed. They all gave their names and address to be kept on file in regards to the murder on that night. They were all hauled out and the nightclub shut down as a major crime scene.

"Doug, who could that have been?" Wanda asked him.

"I don't know, but I'm curious as to who it was myself," he responded.

"One thing's for sure, we don't have to worry about that fake marriage license now," she said.

"I know, but I feel so bad that it happened," he said.

"Well… the night was going too good," Yvonne said.

"That's how it normally goes," Mimi responded.

"I wonder how long they're going to keep us shut down a couple of days?" Yvonne responded.

"I don't know, but it could be weeks. However, you don't have to worry, I got your back. You won't lose anything," Doug informed her.

"I wanna know who that was behind that stage," Mike shouted.

"All I could see was a figure and the gun," Doug said.

"That's all I could see too," Wanda added.

"Could you tell if they were male or female?" Wanda asked.

"No, I couldn't," Doug said.

"Who was missing that you invited?" Wanda asked.

"I checked the list and everyone on it was still in the club when the police arrived," he responded.

"That's odd…cause my list was there too," she shot back.

"I'm really curious now, someone became a ghost. And we don't have a clue who it could possibly be at this point…that scares me," he said.

"Let me see your list, I want to compare it to mine as I check them off," Wanda said as Doug handed her the list.

"Did ya'll tell the detectives about the list?" Yvonne asked them.

"No…I didn't think about it," she said.

"They never asked," Doug responded.

"Then don't mention it now…cause they might charge you with withholding evidence," she informed them.

"Let's see…we both have the same amount so that means everyone was accounted for baby," she told him.

"I know…I checked off Mike, Rita, Kiana, her husband, Alicia, Cassandra, her husband, Dr. Williams, Tenita, her husband, Veronica, Calvin, Sonya, Michelle of course, Mimi, Yvonne, Wanda and myself which made it complete."

"Then who the hell was back there," Mickey asked.

"That's what we're trying to figure out," Mimi said bluntly.

"The police found a black ski mask in the rear of the night club that I saw them confiscate as evidence," Yvonne said.

"I'm sure that was what they were wearing," Doug said.

"Yeah, it was black," Wanda added.

"Well, there's no need of us staying out here. The sun is coming up. Let's go home," Doug insisted to everyone.

"That's a good idea," Mickey responded.

"I'm tired and exhausted myself," Mimi added.

"I could use some rest," Yvonne said sleepily.

"I'll vouch for that," Kiana said.

"I'm out of here," Calvin shouted as Alicia followed.

"I need a ride home," Veronica said loudly.

"Come on ride with me," Mickey offered.

"We'll see ya'll later," Tenita said as she and her husband pulled off. Sonya and her mother left the same time. As Cassandra followed them out the parking lot, Kiana and her husband pulled off too. Rita and Mike left simultaneously. As Doug, Wanda and Yvonne got in their cars, Mimi sped out. Everyone was headed home. Doug thought about the scenario all the way home. When suddenly he noticed that same blue Firebird following him again. As he pulled into the estate, he was really curious as to who the person behind the shooting was. Now he had to find out the next time he sees that car. As they entered the house, Wanda noticed that Doug had a sense of uneasiness about him.

"Are you alright?" she asked him.

"I got a funny feeling about this blue Firebird that keeps following me and every time I attempt to see who it is they disappear," He told her.

"I don't understand," she said.

"On my way here, I spotted it again," he told her.

"Why didn't you say anything?" she asked him.

"I didn't feel there was any need to alarm you. Besides, you weren't involved," he informed her.

"When it concerns you, I'm involved. So I hope you will let me know the next time. They could easily be following me and I would never know it. So I need to know," she told him.

"Alright… I will the next time just in case," he told her.

"When was the first time you noticed it," she asked.

"A few years ago, they appear in spells. I even saw them at my cousin's funeral," he said.

"Then at least you know they been knowing you for quite a while. You may be able to narrow it down from there," she informed him.

"That's a good point," he said thinking.

"Now concentrate on it because it's obvious they are not trying to harm you or they would've done it by now, since they know where you stay," she said looking serious.

"Maybe we do need to inform the detectives about your guest list," he said.

"How is that going to look now?" she asked him.

"I'm not sure," he told her.

"Then you might want to think twice before you make that decision," she told him.

"I must say you do have a point, but it may help them in their investigation to figure out something we couldn't or might've missed," he informed her.

"I'll call them later today…right now I'm tired," he said. As they both headed for bed after a long and draining night at the club, Doug questioned whether he should've had the party. They both contemplated how they were going to figure out who that person was *"Behind the Mask."*

COMING SOON

FALSE
When Two Brothers Go Head To Head!

COMING SOON
A WHORES CONSCIENCE
COVER REVEAL SOON!

SEND MONEY ORDER/CHECK TO:	WYNN PUBLICATIONS P.O. Box 40411 2777 Brentwood RD. Raleigh, NC 27604		
NAME			
ADDRESS			
CITY			
STATE	ZIP		
EMAIL			

BOOK TITLE	PRICE EACH	QUANTITY	TOTAL
BEHIND THE MASK	12.00		
FALSE	12.00		
MY BROTHERS KEEPER PT 1	12.00		
MY BROTHERS KEEPER PT 2	12.00		

	TOTAL	
THANK YOU FOR YOUR BUSINESS	SHIPPING & HANDLING	6.00
	FINAL TOTAL	

www.ingramcontent.com/pod-product-compliance
Lightning Source LLC
Chambersburg PA
CBHW051516170626
46811CB00002B/853